C000194321

THE BLACK BOOK OF ARABIA

Dear Nabel,

Live, Love, Learn,

Hend.

THE BLACK BOOK
OF ARABIA

Hend Al Qassemi

Bloomsbury Qatar Foundation Publishing
P O Box 5825
Doha, Qatar

www.bqfp.com.qa

British Library Cataloguing-in-Publication Data
A catalogue record for this book is available from the British Library.

ISBN: PB: 9789927118098
ePub: 9789927118104

4 6 8 10 9 7 5 3

Typeset by Newgen Knowledge Works (P) Ltd., Chennai, India
Printed and bound in Great Britain by
CPI Group (UK) Ltd, Croydon CR0 4YY

To find out more about our authors and books visit www.bqfp.com.qa.
Here you will find extracts, author interviews, details of forthcoming
events and the option to sign up for our newsletters.

I dedicate this book to my father, a doctor, who taught me that hard work pays off; to my mother, the school principal, who taught me perseverance; and to my beloved grandmother who taught herself to read and write when I was ten. I hope my book inspires us all to be better than yesterday and stronger for those we love.

CONTENTS

Yours Truly

S ARA GAVE BIRTH TO her three daughters—the eldest child followed by twins—back to back, barely a few months apart. The unplanned babies, high pregnancy hormones, and exploding from a size eight to a size sixteen had left Sara with zero self-esteem and confidence. Her marriage, as it were, had evolved into a flurry of daily activities that kept her preoccupied at every turn. Between housework, extended family obligations, and her children, at twenty-six years old Sara enjoyed very little time for herself.

Charming and enchanting, Sara had once held the world at her sumptuously manicured fingertips; now she could not rest easy. She had gone from being a highly organized, competitive manager who dressed to impress and who could summon an employee's best efforts with a radiant smile and a well-placed compliment, to being a housewife whose body paid no heed to diets and whose hormones made her feel defeated, challenged, weak, and needy. Perhaps it was her need for recognition or perhaps it was her longing for a time when obligations and duty did not trump desires and dreams but Sara frequently found herself pondering the ways her beloved husband Ali could or would betray her.

As soon as she would wake, without realizing it, she would find herself imagining Ali eyeing another women—a business associate, a coworker, a retail clerk. In the afternoon, anger would boil up as she pictured him in a tête-à-tête with a mysterious, attractive woman, huddled closely, stealing whispers and smiling languidly with hooded eyes. As each day came to an end, Sara fell into bed after feeding her babies, exhausted by her inner turmoil and battling her doubts and demons, ready to wake every few hours to feed and change her eldest child, aged sixteen months, and her colicky four-month-old twins.

Ali, Sara's husband, had warm hazel eyes and towered at six feet two inches tall partly owing to his German mother. He had always been an attentive husband and was looked up to at the office. His hair was brown, and he wore it short. His facial hair was trimmed to minimum stubble, which suited him. He had dimples when he smiled, making him seem like a gentle giant. He was a light conversationalist, full of support and recognition for any effort done for him. As a result, people always wanted to be around him. He was the envy of many due to his unrivaled charisma and his particular sensitivity toward people. Magnetism at its best. Ali also was a good husband and father, the kind of man who would carry pictures of his daughters in his wallet and whose face would light up when he talked about them.

While Sara felt an endless love for her brood, she resented the toll that the long and hard journey of pregnancy had taken on her body. Her once-tight stomach was now a "kangaroo pouch" of loose skin that hung around her hips.

The stretch marks on her stomach were like a road map of shiny jagged silver lines. She tried to remove them with creams from Sephora, rich cocoa butter-and-chemical concoctions that had received high customer satisfaction ratings in international fashion columns, blogs, and journals. The lines decreased in color, but they still gleamed a fluorescent whitish-gray every time Sara switched on the light in the bathroom's full-length mirror. The scars of pregnancy. Her vanity suffered a daily blow, and her racks of silhouette-emphasizing clothes started to collect dust.

Sara would stand for hours in front of the mirror, reminiscing about her past glory only to walk away with a sinking feeling of defeat and disgust, the same feeling that caused her to shrink from her husband's touch every time he reached out for her. She did not want him to feel her empty sack of loose skin.

It did not help that three different plastic surgeons had refused to perform a restorative procedure to her abdomen, advising her—begging her—to lose some weight on her own to allow them to do a better job. It had only been four months since she gave birth, and that was too soon, they said. Surgery was best done after she was finished having children. They advised a grace period of another three to six months to allow the body to regain its shape, but Sara was deaf to this.

As much hype as there was for fashions for the happy mother-to-be, there was absolutely nothing for the post-delivery mom. Sara was left staring at her old slim-fit fashions and the clothes she had worn when she felt like a pregnant hippopotamus. Naturally, she would choose the loose-fitting clothes because they were comfortable and allowed for a quick breastfeed without too much trouble. The comfort factor masked her size. She pined for the old days.

Sara also had developed freckles and blotchy areas of darkened skin known as mask of pregnancy on her face. Women with darker complexions are more prone to this condition, which becomes more pronounced with each pregnancy. Sara struggled to find creams to lighten her skin because she disliked the comments that her husband was fairer-skinned than she was. Once, when traveling with Ali during their honeymoon, someone asked where they were from, observing that Ali looked European while she did not. "His mom is German," Sara replied. "I guess that helps." One European lady once asked, "Are you Indian or African?"

Ali told Sara that the changes to her body did not matter, but she did not believe him. He thought she was simply suffering the postpartum blues. He even took the time to read about it, because her depressive isolation was affecting him. He felt partially to blame for her condition, believing they should have spaced out the pregnancies to better allow her body time to return to its previous shape.

In bed, if Ali casually stretched his arm out to his wife, his touch would be rebuffed as if he had electrocuted her, scaring him to the point that he began to worry that he might accidentally brush against her while tossing or turning. He knew she was nervous and physically unhappy, but understood that she had just borne him his pride and joy. He missed the intimacy they once shared. It hurt that she refused to sleep with him, but he simply thought that she perhaps needed time to accept her shape, or that she would fix her body with diet and exercise as she had done before. However, with three children under two years old, Sara never had the time to establish an exercise regimen. At night she was grateful if she had a few hours of sleep to allow her not to doze off during meals or while taking care of the children.

Sara tried to lose weight, but diets backfired, exercise depleted her energy, and her children and housework dominated every waking minute. She breastfed because her babies had sensitive stomachs and baby formula induced colic. Breastfeeding allowed her to sleep longer and rest better, but it also made her hungry in an angry way, to the extent that her stomach would hurt if she did not eat to her heart's content. But if she gave the babies the artificial milk, their gentle stomachs would ache and they would keep her up at night wailing.

Sara's mother, blessed with a youthful figure that she worked hard to maintain, taunted Sara about her weight gain. She said she was only trying to motivate Sara to return to her old self, but she could not quite mask the tone of superiority and, perhaps, secret pleasure in her voice. Sara's father reminded her like clockwork of how she had once wanted to model in school shows, wear her own designs in photo shoots, and explored being a fashion blogger. His jokes struck sensitive chords that no one but she could hear. Her friends sent her pictures that would infuriate her, snapshots from past parties, weddings, and days out when she was the fittest of the bunch. It was easier to isolate herself than to explain to everyone that she was having a difficult time coming to terms with her new life and shape. The world simply refused to accept the new her, and that made it difficult for her to accept herself.

With colicky babies and a growing toddler blurting out new words at every turn, Sara found herself drowning in self-doubt. Unable to appreciate her husband's many attempts to alleviate her stress, she felt frazzled and overwhelmed. She avoided him at home and more so in bed. The fire of discontent burned deep inside. She would look at herself in the mirror on the medicine cabinet and, seeing dark circles around her eyes, wrinkles, freckles, dark patches, and capillaries, would ask herself why her husband would want to be with her. She was ugly now. It was ridiculous how she used to fret over a few kilos but now had an extra twenty-five. She felt like a large object and did not want to be seen.

"A fat cow," she said one night in bed. "That's what I've become. You don't like me anymore."

"What do you mean?" asked Ali. Half asleep, he thought she was referring to feeding the babies cow's milk, because she had been talking about different kinds of baby formula that gave babies colic and how she had researched lactose-free milk, goat milk, and soya milk, and found they were better.

"I'm ugly. I hate myself and I hate what I've become. I feel like a barrel. I have to get everything tailored to fit me." Her voice broke. A silent tear found its way down her face, unnoticed and ignored.

"Honey, you just had a baby. Give it time. You had twins. One baby is a big job. You're doing two jobs, and you're just one person." Ali paused. "Let's go away for a weekend," he suggested, thinking that a bit of travel could change Sara's mood.

"And what am I going to do with the babies?" She began yelling. "My breasts will burst if I leave the children behind, and I can't depend on anyone to handle them. Every time my mother or your mother decides to help, they mess up their sleeping patterns, and I end up suffering with grumpy babies!"

Silence. He had tried to help; he had failed. *Women are impossible to please*, he thought. They simply spoke a different language or accent and too much was lost in translation. Spoil them and they will love you, they say. It had never worked for him. Ever. When he offered to have his mother help, Sara called him a momma's boy. If he offered to allow his mother-in-law to help, Sara said he was siding with her mother. When he suggested a wet nurse to help with feeding the babies, Sara labeled him as "spendy" and told him they would never be able to build their dream house. Impossible to please was one of the definitions of women. Ali just wanted to get as much sleep as he could before the alarm went off. He worked hard and needed the rest. He was a man, and he tried to be fair. He wished that she would indulge his misunderstandings, which were entirely unintentional anyway.

Gradually and secretly, Sara's fear of losing her husband consumed her. She was scared. It was no longer a matter of if, but of when, where, and how. When Ali failed to answer her phone calls, she pictured him in a hotel with another woman, pushing the elevator button, walking her to a room, showing her a luxurious suite overlooking the city. She imagined him standing behind her as she gazed out the window, red roses in his hand, the city at her feet. He would leave Sara and her babies because she was no longer as pretty as she once had been. The scenes and feelings were so real that Sara felt she was not imagining them but actually seeing them as they occurred. The fires of suspicion raged, consuming her waking hours. She had too much time with the babies and no company but her demons.

She grew determined to prove once and for all that Ali, a seemingly loving husband and doting father, was in fact a lying, cheating, deceitful man. The coals were there, and she just needed to turn them for the fire to rage wildly. After all, aren't all men looking for the perfect woman? Why should he be patient with her while she failed to restore her figure and glamour? It was just a matter of time, and she could not simply sit around and wait for some home wrecker to steal her happiness.

Sara imagined the many ways in which she could put Ali to the test. In her mind, there was no better way to find out if he coveted the grass on the other side than to tempt him with another woman. But who? She was embarrassed to confide her fears to her friends. After disappearing from the social calendar and not returning their calls, how could she contact them out of the blue, and with such an indecent proposal? They would not understand her fear, her need to know that she was still beautiful in Ali's eyes. She shivered at the thought of how they would laugh at her. Besides, there were too many stories of such attempts that backfired with the husband marrying the bait. She could not risk it. She thought about hiring someone to carry out the plan, a professional, but that could leave a money trail. If the temptress succeeded, she might demand more money, blackmailing Sara with the threat of exposing what she had done to her husband. No, it had to be someone she could trust.

When at last the solution presented itself, it was obvious: She would do it herself. And it would be easy. Simple. Clear. Clean. Foolproof. Blackmail-free. The smart way to do it. She would set the trap by being the other woman herself. *Plain and simple genius,* she thought to herself. She toyed with the idea until it became her only delightful hobby, until she was giddy with frivolous excitement. She applauded herself for concocting such a devious plan and sat smiling as the babies nursed and slept peacefully.

She bought a mobile number, created fake Facebook and WhatsApp accounts, and began to lure her husband into "speaking" to her. Naturally, since he would recognize her voice, she only sent text messages. To separate herself from online scammers and to gain his confidence, she sent him quotes and mottoes he was fond of, including posters she found online with beautiful images and the words he favored.

Waste no more time arguing about what a good man should be. Be one.

and

I don't count my sit-ups. I only start counting when it starts hurting. That is when I start counting, because then it really counts. That's what makes you a champion.

Sara knew what Ali liked in a woman and exactly which buttons to push to spark his interest, making it that much easier to spin her web, confident he would eventually fall into it with abandon, however long it took. It was fun rediscovering ways of enticing her husband, harassing him, and playing games with his heart. She felt like a woman again. It excited her and made her forget the cramps in her lower abdomen every time she stood up suddenly. It made her forget that she did not feel attractive. It gave her such an ego boost that she would crave it. There is a certain pleasure in sinning and in knowing you have the upper hand and the control to walk away whenever you want.

But as well-conceived as these overtures were, Ali never responded to them. Instead of taking consolation in his disinterest and fidelity, Sara became aggravated. With stubborn determination she persisted. She spent hours a day finding news items, images, and sayings to intrigue him. Nothing worked. The challenge had begun; it was either him or her, and she was always right.

Desperate to gain his attention, she used her phone to send him a "selfie" that was actually a picture of a magazine page with a model's alluring eyes looking out from a veil. She chose a Latin-looking model and saved several different shots of her in her phone's memory to be presented to him as bait in the future. He had always liked the sun-kissed look.

She moved into another bedroom to create a fertile ecosystem in which to stray and possibly fall as Adam had. Ali never responded to her messages and her gentle, persistent enticing, but Sara's stubborn nature insisted that she had to be right in the end. She created a character who was an attractive, strong, fun woman who was hopelessly in love with Ali. All she wanted was communication. He didn't have to reply in kind; she just wanted to know that he received her messages. Finally, after months of ignoring her, Ali responded.

As soon as he did, his caring chat mate wanted to know if he was all right. Had he had his breakfast? How was he feeling? What was he doing? Exhilarated but careful not to overreact, Sara proceeded cautiously. As badly as she wanted to put Ali to the final test, she made small talk at first. The shower of attention continued for months. Sara began to receive more and more texts and emails from Ali as he sought solace and comfort with "Tamara." Slowly and persistently, she managed to turn his abrupt responses into sentences and, eventually, paragraphs.

She was Tamara, a lonely but educated and beautiful woman. Not surprisingly, their discussions turned toward his marriage. How long had he been married? Was he happy? Satisfied? The first few times the topic came up, Ali professed happiness, but with a little prodding he finally complained that his wife had changed. Sara was still a great mother, to be sure, but as a wife she was absent. And while his wife closed herself off, mourning her lost beauty and fanning the flame of suspicion, Ali found with Tamara what he lacked with Sara. She allowed it, because she wanted to see if he was hungry enough to cheat. He complained that his wife never had time for him anymore, but she secretly basked in the hours he spent with her online. For in Sara's mind, a man spent time on what he valued most, be it his friends, wife, lover, children, work, or even a hobby such as fishing or socializing with other men in the *majlis*. If a man spent time with you, he was sacrificing his time elsewhere for your sake. When he avoided you, he was simply not interested anymore in what you had to say, give, or do. Now Ali was spending hours online with her.

Tamara boldly asked what kind of intimacy he missed. Ali disclosed some of the things his wife did that he enjoyed. Sara was flattered to hear how much Ali appreciated what she did for him but she was angry that he discussed them openly with this online stranger. Tamara asked about his fantasies. He was too shy to tell them to Sara, but, protected by distance, he told Tamara everything. Even in his betrayal he was thinking of Sara; she could tell he was describing her, not as she was before the children, but as she was now. Sara smiled to think how easy it would be to make her husband happy, but she let Tamara promise it instead. Tamara not only would do those things, but she wanted to do them; she craved doing them. She exercised her wildest imaginings on him, and more. She taunted and toyed with him, and she made him laugh. He enjoyed the conversations and he expressed himself openly with her. He wrote how wonderful she was and how he wished they could meet, speak, and be together.

Tamara knew him well. She had studied him intently over the years. The outcome of a sporting event he followed, a new song by a favorite singer, a recent movie with an actor or actress he liked—all were fodder for conversation and connection. She painted a picture of sharing such things together, and Ali responded. She masterminded the soul mate whose company he would enjoy. He liked to take care of the woman he was with and be appreciated for it. His simple acts of texting her when waking, when he arrived at work, and during meals were important to him, although she never understood why. The messages seemed repetitive, but Sara played the role well and continued to chirp *Sweet mornings* and *Sweet dreams* to him, throwing in a line of poetry or an intriguing quote.

The gratification Sara felt every time he replied slowly began to fill her with the not-so-foreign emotions of a passion that she had lost. When Ali was home, she found herself becoming dull because every time she thought of something interesting or witty to say, she would save it for Tamara. When he was gone, she searched the Internet for tidbits that Tamara could share on her Facebook page or in private messages. He did not respond to every post or text, but when he did, she luxuriated in his attention. It was like courting a prince, but more than a prince, because he was her lifelong love.

Intense and encompassing, the feeling stopped short every time she realized that his need and comfort were with Tamara, not with her. It did not matter that she was both. What had started out as a small and harmless test of fidelity had become a living nightmare that dominated every minute of her day. The elation Sara felt as Tamara gained Ali's attention and affection never quite matched the disappointment she felt as she watched her husband slipping away, chat by chat, word by word, emoticon by emoticon.

Sara wanted to end it. But the more contact they had, the harder it became to retract it all. More importantly, how was she to explain that she had done it to prove that he would cheat? His pride would never stand it, and neither would hers. She wanted to put him to the test. Would he meet her? Sleep with her? Marry her? Would he forget that he had a wife who had borne him three children? Who was once pretty and could possibly go back to being fit one day? Even if she was going through an emotionally unstable stage and was overly suspicious?

Ali pushed to meet Tamara in person, to taste the forbidden fruit at last. He texted. He sent private emails. He pursued Tamara with the same passion with which he had pursued Sara a few years earlier. Talking to him over the phone would blow her cover, so Tamara refused to speak to him while Sara was still his wife. She said she would only do it after he divorced her, which he point blank refused to do. That stopped her heart, but she was beginning to feel that she had created a monster. The fruit of her loins,

Tamara, had grown into a woman who controlled Ali and tested him in terms of money and marriage. He sent her money by the wads and offered her marriage, but would never leave his wife and children.

She avoided responding. He kept texting her. She tried to discourage him by criticizing things he liked, saying things she knew would annoy him, discussing topics of no interest to him. Nothing seemed to work. The differences seemed only to add piquancy to the relationship. It was getting out of control and she tried everything to end it, to turn him away, even distastefully, all to no avail. She could see him hurting at home as he turned away from food and languished by the day. His emails to Tamara burned her eyes to read:

Tamara, my one and my all,

In losing myself to your love, I have found my lost soul. A soul I would never have known had I not stumbled and fallen in love with you. Hopelessly, truly and deeply. All that I desire is to fulfill my love for you. I am a man of my word, and I have so much to say to you. If I cannot say it or express myself to you, I feel as though I will die suffocating.

In your love your sun has blinded me, but I cannot see at night. I see colors I do not know the names of. And should I die, I will beg my wife to bring you to my grave because my bones desire you to step on my remains. I want you in my life, and in my death. You needn't bring roses, for you are the rosiest rose in the garden of my sight, and your thorns have made my heart bleed after you have disappeared.

I would offer you the world, but you say you have your own. What can I give you that can make you want me? I do not want to live a day without you in my life. Isn't it crazy that the only time I can bear to smile is when I think of you?

I only miss you when I am breathing.

Run away with me. Please <3

It was now Ali's turn in the valley of lost souls. His eyes became glassy and he lost weight. His short, dirty beard became an unkempt two-week-old beard more out of a lack of interest than out of religious or fashion notions. He did not care how he looked anymore, and he looked almost fragile. When asked, he would blame it on the stress at work. Sara invited his sisters and parents to visit in hopes of cheering him up. Everyone noticed that Ali was no longer Ali. It was as if an alien had abducted him and he was a mere shell of the person he once had been.

At home, Sara stopped being distant, offering herself to her husband and tempting him with the fantasies he had confided in Tamara. It was no use. Ali was in love with Tamara, and nothing Sara could do or say would change his feelings for her. Tamara was ruthless and compassionate all at once. She was his savior and his temptress, everything that he wanted and needed. He would never see her, and he sat there apathetically and moped. He would cry in the bathroom, and Sara could hear him while he let the shower run. He was quick to notice something pretty on his wife and inquire where she bought it, to secretly buy it and send it to his beloved Tamara. In the beginning it was funny, then fascinating to see how far he would stretch to nurture this budding affair. He would bend over backwards and sideways in his attempts to charm and captivate Tamara. Sara kept stock of the items he sent, planning to one day reveal to him how much money he had wasted on his online girlfriend; but when the items became more expensive, her sweet game turned sour, and, if exposed, would leave a bad aftertaste in everyone's mouth.

His texts kept coming.

I need you.
I will die without you . . .
How can you do this to me?
Have you no heart. </3
Ask me for anything and it is yours—just please come back.

Sara stopped replying to him. She removed the chip from her phone and burned it for fear he might find out who Tamara really was. He would never forgive her if she admitted the truth.

She brought her daughters to Ali's office to celebrate his "Surprise Happy Un-Birthday," thinking it entertaining and fun for the whole family. She wanted him back in her life. She regretted putting her plan into action and she prayed she would be able to undo what she had done. She would fix it. Her body had slimmed down, and she was over her depression.

He hugged and kissed his daughters and thanked his wife politely but with no emotion or even the trace of a smile in his voice. When the party turned quiet, he excused himself to step outside, sit under a tree, and send Tamara more messages in yet another attempt to reawaken his absent love.

It had been almost a month since Sara had removed the chip from the phone. He pined for Tamara, and Sara suffered. She acted ignorant of his withering state of health and heart and attempted to play his favorite Egyptian comedies and American soaps, but he would sit staring at the screen unmoved, untouched, emotionally paralyzed.

What have I done? she thought. She prayed to God to help her, to guide her, to forgive her for what she had done to the man she loved. "I am so sorry. I don't know why I did it," she prayed. "He didn't deserve to suffer like this. I love him so very much, and I can't see my life without him. I want to make it up to him."

He walked about the house deathlike and stopped eating and sleeping normally. He became socially autistic, having no communication with anyone, and absentminded. Once they found him sleeping in the car with his hand hugging his mobile. It was like watching a drug addict cut off from all drugs. The withdrawal symptoms were scary to watch. Usually drug abusers are provided with therapists and antidepressants; all Ali had were the haunted messages of his former love. Tamara was his morphine, his obsession, his fix, and now she was gone. The veil of mystery that surrounded her kept him from any sin or hurt or dissatisfaction, because, simply put, he had never seen her.

She had simply been taunting, teasing, and provoking his emotions with no intention of satisfying his curiosity. It fueled an unkind, maddening craving in him, and his open, sensitive nature left him unprotected from its ravages. He could not understand why Tamara had disappeared. She came to him in his dreams, and he would wake up weeping like a baby.

Having pledged never to leave his wife and to remain faithful and true, Ali, desperate and confused, would quietly cry himself to sleep as Sara listened. In the morning, with dark circles under his eyes, he dragged his feet as he got ready to go to work. Before he left, he would hug his babies as if he was worried he would die before he returned. It was heartbreaking to watch, especially for someone who was once such an inspirational thinker and aggressively enterprising businessman.

Unable to admit the truth, Tamara sent him one last email telling him to stop, that it was unfair to his wife, unfair to his children, and unfair to her. This would be the last message he would receive from her. She said she was going to study at Harvard University to get a Master of Business Administration. She had lost interest in him because he was married and tied down with children. She did not want his "baggage." She wanted to explore her life and build her career. It was a cruel email, but as they say, sometimes you have to be cruel to be kind.

Within minutes Ali's response arrived in her inbox. He had divorced Sara. He was a free man. He was ready to marry her.

He sent Tamara an email with the divorce contract attached in a last attempt to prove his love for her. He had left her as promised. He was hers at last.

Sara called Ali, but he ignored her calls. He was waiting for Tamara to call. Surely she would be eager to be with him now that he was free. They loved each other. She understood him better than his own wife did. He needed her in order to be happy, and he believed in her with such fierce adoration that for her to fail him would be like the sun failing to shine the next day.

Sara rushed to the bedroom. All of Ali's cabinets had been emptied. She ran downstairs to the garage. His car was missing. He had gone. He had left her for another woman.

He had left her for her.

★ ★ ★

Dear Sara,

I never knew I had a wild heart, but now I do, and wild hearts cannot be tamed. I tried to stop myself, but I had to say goodbye. You will receive everything you need and my girls will want for nothing. But I am in love, and this love has broken me. I did not choose this state of heart, mind, and soul; it chose me.

Perhaps I was weak. Perhaps her love sated me during my days of drought from you. I don't want to blame you or blame myself. All I want to say is that my heart has chosen another, and you are free to choose who you want to be with, as am I.

I haven't cheated on you, but I cannot be with you anymore because the Angel of Death visits me five times a day. Every time I lower my head in prayer, I cannot help beseeching my God to give her to me. When I rest my head on the mat, my heart breaks that I call for her to be praying next to me. They say we are allowed four wives, but my heart can only hold one powerful love. She has my heart.

I have struggled to come to terms with what is right and wrong. She is everything that is right with the world, and yet she is everything that is wrong with me, because I am not with her.

She is the love I never believed could exist, the poem I never knew how to write, and the story I have always wanted to live. Every time I say goodbye to her, I die a little. I learned that to truly love is to allow myself to be vulnerable. I did this to myself, I admit it. But Sara, I want to allow it because this love has made me feel alive. This is the real thing. It is everything I ever wanted and will ever need.

I am moving to America to study and begin a new life. I hope you can find it within your heart to forgive me and move on. I wish you the best and I hope that we each get what we deserve in this life.

Yours truly,
Ali

The Princess and the Pauper

L ulu's father was from the south of Saudi Arabia, Najran, but moved to Riyadh after marrying his cousin Fatima, who lived in the capital. He sold camels, sheep, and goats, which was a lucrative trade in the region, although it was regarded as slightly primitive, showing how limited in their thinking and how traditional these people were. Her father was stingy, would haggle where and when he could, and was always interested in making deals and cutting corners. Some of his camels would fetch millions of Saudi riyals, yet he still collected their manure and sold it as fertilizer.

Fatima bore him eight children: three girls and five boys. When the children were older, she opened a beauty salon in the Al Takhasussi and Al Aliya area. It gained a reputation as a prestigious salon and afforded her the opportunity to meet women from different backgrounds. After two years, she was steadily making money and friends in high society.

One day a tall, plain-looking Moroccan woman in her late twenties and dressed in an old abaya came in and asked for work. Having no experience or training in the beauty profession, she was of no use so Fatima politely refused her. The woman said she would work for minimum wage and did not mind starting at the bottom as long as she could sleep in the salon after work hours and earn an honest living. She stayed in the salon even after receiving her rejection, trying to make herself useful by picking up behind customers, cleaning, and complimenting customers on their hair or whichever service they had come in for. It was irritating yet heartbreaking to witness her desperation, so Fatima eventually gave in, allowing the woman to work for minimum wage and sleep in the salon until they could figure out which job or service best suited her.

Hadeya, the Moroccan, worked hard, and soon began to learn the ways of professional beauty care. She realized that the hairdressers earned the most money, as opposed to the employees, who were mostly lower-paid Filipinos, that gave massages, helped with the scrubbing at the Moroccan baths, gave facials, waxed, or provided nail care. Hair was the final touch, which could take a long time to finish, but would be the crowning glory of any girl aiming to dazzle and shine. The best tips were also in the hair business, especially home services, which was a double rate charge and tips were multiplied.

Eventually, Hadeya picked up hair styling and coloring, advancing quickly to the point where she even styled Fatima's hair. She did so well and was such a pleasure to work with that she was invited to Fatima's house to do both her and her husband's hair.

Within a year, Fatima was divorced, and ownership of her property, which had been under her husband's name, was now under Hadeya's. The camel herder had divorced his wife of twenty-seven years and turned her out into the streets in the middle of the night, informing her that he was to marry Hadeya. When his wife started to quarrel, he simply and quietly told her that he had divorced her that morning, then handed her the papers and told her to leave.

Heartbroken, the sudden divorcee went to live with her second son and wife, who eventually built her an independent house on his home grounds. But the "midnight divorce," as it had come to be known, was a scandal that was never forgotten. The salon was boycotted for a while, but eventually its convenience, familiarity, and fantastic location took precedence over everything else, and everyone wanted to know how and what Hadeya had done to get a rich and mature man to give up his partner of many years to marry the help.

Lulu was the product of this notorious union. She and her siblings were treated as the children of sin, the seed of a home wrecker. Mothers would instruct their children not to have lunch with Lulu or her siblings for fear of consuming anything concocted with black magic. As a result, other children would ask Hadeya's children not to hurt them or to share their magic tricks. Lulu and her younger sisters and brother would smile or act like they did not understand, because acknowledging what was said was more painful. Sometimes they would defend themselves and their mother, but no one paid attention because they already had an opinion of them.

Their classmates had Lebanese, Iraqi, Syrian, Algerian, and Moroccan mothers married to Saudi men, but they did not suffer the same discrimination that Lulu did, and she resented it. She blamed her mother for her stigma and never forgave her for her dishonorable entry into her marriage. The situation made it difficult for Lulu to make friends and undoubtedly would make it nearly impossible to find a suitable husband in the future. The other children of Moroccan mothers would even go so far as to avoid her because they said she gave all Moroccans a bad name. Lulu felt suffocated by the prejudice against her and yearned to leave the country in order to escape it all. She wanted to enjoy more liberty, far from Saudi Arabia's strict rules prohibiting women from driving and requiring them to cover, and its lack of entertainment. She wanted people to think that she was like her friends, from a normal Saudi family, or as she would often insinuate, a royal. If people laughed at her or mocked her, she would say that eventually she would be a princess. If her mother was smart enough to snare a Saudi, she was smart enough to snag a prince! She was a failure in her studies, and was on the heavy side of the scales. But she would pacify herself by saying that men liked heavier women anyway.

Lulu never overcame the condescending manner in which people regarded her. The scandal was quite dramatic and all the more celebrated in disgust and envy because Hadeya was running a successful, inexpensive salon. People continued to criticize Lulu's father for marrying a woman who bit the hand that not only fed her but also had given her a home and the skills to earn a livelihood. But Lulu's father, now seventy years old, put all of his wealth in the names of his new wife and her children, so the eight children from his first marriage would inherit nothing after he passed away. Hadeya came up with the plan, saying that she feared his orphans would be attacked after her wall was gone. And so he arranged for all his wealth and property to go to the children of his new, beloved wife. He even bought the building that housed the salon and registered it in Lulu's name.

Lulu often voiced her embarrassment and bitter resentment to her nanny, a Moroccan of Berber origin. Her nanny was fat, tall, extremely loving, and always forgiving of her spoiled little mistress, who she had raised since she was three years old. The nanny knew everything there was to know about Lulu—from her good nature with those she loved to the bad that she was capable of doing. When the nanny was forty-five, a suitable suitor proposed, and she decided to wed before it was too late. Lulu never forgave her loving confidante for leaving her, regarding her nanny's actions as some form of treachery and never spoke to her again. In a way, Lulu saw in the nanny someone more worthy than her mother to bear the title of "mother," and Lulu felt that in deciding to get married her nanny had given up on her "child."

At five foot, two inches tall and seventy-four kilograms, Lulu was as round as someone who ate three fast-food meals a day would be expected to be. She could not move fast or find clothes that fit her off the rack. She had to buy oversized trousers to allow for her lower abdomen and torso and then trim the bottom for her short height. Elastic leggings and T-shirts were her favorite outfit, the one-size-fits-all dress code. She desperately wanted to marry someone of a princely stature, but no one would have her. She was too short, too fat, and too lacking in her studies. She was incapable of striking up an intriguing enough conversation for a man to inquire after her or even to call.

She wanted to get a world-class education and meet the kind of people who would lift her up and eventually allow her to marry into the very society that excluded her from their activities and social gatherings. She wanted to be made exceptional, elite in any way or form that she could. She was willing to buy it, to cheat for it, to skim, to work, or to study for it even though she knew herself to be a hopeless student.

Working in the salon was a chore, and she longed to be served instead of serving people. Every sunrise was the start of a new battle between herself and her reality. It was degrading to be doing menial work when she went to an elite school, though she did not know the first thing about speaking in millions or leaving an unfinished croissant on her plate. Her father had millions but would give her only enough for a single, cheap meal, and she always finished whatever she had to eat—which was fast food only and always. She went to the same schools as the elite girls she

28

admired, spoke with their Arabic accent, and learned their good and bad habits. Yet, however much she tried she was disregarded and disconnected when and where it counted. She battled her demons but never lost hope. For after all, if her mother, a low-paid immigrant could do it, she surely had better options.

Lulu's English-language skills were weak, and she passed only with much bribery and gifts. She struggled to switch from pen and paper to the laptop and smart technology that her classmates so easily mastered. However, she never surrendered to her lack of linguistic knowledge and was accepted as a silent guest since she never hurt anyone. She just wanted to be one of the girls. Still, a tornado stirred in her whenever she lounged with the socialites; half the class was made up of princesses and the other half was from the richest families of Riyadh.

Most of Lulu's teachers visited the salon, and that proved to be her winning card. She would embarrass them into helping her by refusing to accept payment after serving them. Hadeya, too, was trying her utmost to fit into the society that she was now a part of, sending couscous to the faculty every Friday. She aimed to please, and please she did. Eventually, people forgot about the old boss; Hadeya's cheap rates and prime location on one of Riyadh's busiest streets won over a large clientele. It took years, but Hadeya eventually reached a level of accept-ance within the society that once ignored and disregarded her. Teachers, doctors, high school girls, college students, matchmakers, and housewives of all sorts sat in the salon, sipping Moroccan tea and enjoying the company of the funny Moroccan employees. The clients enjoyed a variety of sweets and shared stories about how to get better skin, hair, and nails and about the beautiful Queen Selma of Morocco, and they swapped cooking recipes.

Lulu's father did not want to send her to Europe or America for further education. She had never been abroad before, it was too expensive, and she had not been accepted into any scholarship programs. He opted to send her to Kuwait to finish her higher studies, as she was adamant about not graduating from a school in Saudi Arabia. Kuwait was cheaper than London or California for the tight-fisted father, and Lulu was his precious first-born from his beloved Hadeya. He wanted to know that she was a short distance away, as opposed to a half-day or full-day trip to a cold country. Lulu was disappointed. All of her friends were traveling abroad for higher education, but she was refused entry to all the foreign universities because of her low grades and poor English proficiency.

Lulu set out for Kuwait brokenhearted, thinking what a difficult task it would be to find the super-rich and super-fabulous in a small state, as opposed to glamorous America where at an Ivy League university she would be handed the opportunity on a silver platter. "The company of giants makes you a giant," her mother used to tell her when she would complain about the children in school. Nevertheless, being away was better than being watched and control-led by her parents, by the conservative Saudi police, and by a strict society and traditions that limited her access to liberal attire and actions. Plus, the travel was interesting and mysteriously inviting.

During her first week in Kuwait at the university dorms, Lulu developed a homesickness that left her crying every night, thinking how much better her schoolmates must be doing under the California sun. She remembered one of her mother's customers from the salon, who had mentioned that she knew a royal from Kuwait, so Lulu asked for an introduction. Perhaps she would make life interesting and replace the royal circle she would sorely miss. Her friend made a few phone calls, and an introduction was made. The royal, Sheikha, called Lulu and welcomed her to Kuwait. It would become "her home away from home," she promised.

Sheikha was an attractive, confident, and successful woman. Born into the royal family of Kuwait, she was blessed with bewitching brown eyes; a fine, straight, slightly aquiline nose; full, shapely lips; and a tall hourglass figure. Lulu enjoyed the affiliation with Sheikha and thought that in due time, even the ladies-in-waiting of such successful people marry well-to-do suitors. With brains to match her beauty, Sheikha had put off marriage until she completed her studies: a Bachelor's degree in Information Technology and a Master of Business Administration in the UK that she planned to use for the launch of her own luxury prod-ucts' retail website. When she finally chose her suitor, hearts were broken and hopes were dashed.

Sheikha enjoyed a whirlwind romance with the young, rich, and handsome prince of her choice. Her close friends enjoyed accompanying her on yacht trips, lavish parties at the trendiest islands, and private jet trips to watch horses race at the most famous racetracks in Europe and America. Sheikha documented the trips in photos that she posted to her group of girlfriends on her BlackBerry Messenger and WhatsApp. Lulu saved all of these images along with the ones she herself took of her friend's lifestyle.

Sheikha's life was cream and honey, as it were; Lulu's life in Saudi Arabia had been vinegar and salt. Lulu had come to Kuwait wanting to study at the American University of Kuwait but did not make the TOEFL score so was not allowed entry. Furthermore, she had come with a group of Saudi friends who deemed her unworthy of their company to begin with, since she was of Bedouin origin and had a mother whose history was tainted. They feared both black magic and her reputation rubbing off on their as-yet single lives.

Sheikha's kind words warmed Lulu's heart, and she was excited when Sheikha invited her to a gathering with a mix of girls from the Gulf, all seniors, who welcomed her to the country and university. Unfortunately, Lulu was too shy to admit to her new friends who were fluent in English that she failed the TOEFL prerequisite and would study at an Arabic university. As the evening went on, however, her new friends discovered that she was not keeping up when they spoke in English, and she broke down. She was scared and nervous, with no mother, no nanny, no father, and no salon services or food provided on speed dial. She was mortified at first, but then let the tears run like rain. Sobbing and seeking pity was a splendid way to introduce yourself to the kind, strong, and brave. She won their hearts as everyone felt sorry for her because she would not stop complaining about how she felt out of place amongst the "uncultured" and "poor" students in her dorm. There were no glam names, no glitzy fashion, no shiny, top-of-the-range cars. The worst thing in this foreign experience was that there were no maids to bring her clothing to her, pay attention to her beauty needs, or handle her waking times, meals, and errands. It was almost cruel, and the culture shock shattered her very being. It was enough for her to attempt suicide, she said, as she was facing social suicide after years of climbing up the social ladder. The girls embraced her, and Sheikha even invited her to spend the weekend in her house. Lulu donned the puss-in-boots façade and sold them the story that she was spoiled for choice in Saudi Arabia and now was in Kuwait, left to fend for herself among the poor and unworthy girls that she deemed beneath her and, in her elite opinion, disgusting.

"My mother and father both went to the same university you aren't liking. It's not for poor or uncultured people," said Sheikha with a smile, trying to cheer her up.

"But I don't know anyone there," Lulu said, her voice breaking. "Everyone looks like they don't know anything about anything. I am a complete stranger there. I can't sleep on their single bed; it is only a meter wide. I swear I keep thinking I'm going to fall off on the tile floor!"

Lulu arrived at Sheikha's with her luggage and never left. Literally. She resided in the lap of luxury. Servants waited on her instead of her having to wait for the shared bathroom and showers at the dorms. She would leave the bathroom a mess—towels tossed on the ground, tissues everywhere but in the bin, and the toothpaste tube left without the cover and oozing. Were it not for the servants regularly cleaning, the next person who entered would have found it rude. Her clothes were always pressed, either ironed or steamed. Buttons sewn on when they fell off or came loose. Accessories fixed when and where necessary. Food served around the clock. Travel expenses were paid and visas issued, in addition to regular expensive gifts from different generous members of the family. This was the life she had dreamed of; save there was no husband, just a kind girl who hosted her. Her dream had come true—she lived in a palace she deemed herself worthy of and enjoyed the luxury she had hoped to attain. The servants served her, as opposed to her picking at the clogged hair at the salon sink after her mother had shut down and the staff had left. She was treated as a member of the family. Money was handed to her on every occasion, and delicious food was served at the ring of a bell. Why would anyone want to leave heaven?

When Lulu's tight-fisted father heard that his daughter was living with a royal, he stopped sending her anything except pocket money, a mere 300 Kuwaiti dinars a month. Lulu received almost tenfold that amount living with Sheikha. The contrast was almost ridiculously cruel in her eyes. She would speak at times about how much money her father had, but how difficult and greedy he was with his hard-earned money. Yet she loved him and hated her mother. She hated that he was tight with money, but she knew he loved her and that after he passed away, she would inherit his money. Her mother, on the other hand, would always be regarded as a husband-snatcher and a common hairdresser at a mid-level salon—even after her death. Lulu longed to be a princess and forget her roots. With Sheikha, she was living her dream.

Lulu's younger sister, Mona, would always tell her that she was learning how to be glamorous from Sheikha. It was true. Lulu regarded Sheikha as her idol and role model, and she copied her in everything she did. Imitation is a form of flattery, they say, and Lulu flattered Sheikha, although she certainly liked to think of herself as already a lady of royal stature. She liked to think of Sheikha as someone worthy of being her mother—not the man-snatcher who was stigmatized or the worthless maid who had abandoned her. Sheikha was a perfect fit, someone she was happy and proud to be affiliated with. In the Arab world they say that after forty days of living with someone, you become one of them. Lulu's stay in Sheikha's household lasted for two years. After failing the first course in the university, Lulu simply stayed with Sheikha—going out with her whenever she did or staying home with her and her family.

Eventually, Lulu overstayed her welcome. She overheard Sheikha's family discussing when she was expected to leave, as taking care of someone else's daughter was a responsibility that was not to be regarded as trivial in the Middle East. Sheikha tried to encourage Lulu to pursue her education, even if at first it was at an institute for English-language beginners. She could work toward a diploma at a university later.

The harder Sheikha tried to convince Lulu to study and obtain some form of degree, the harder Lulu looked for a place to stay after Sheikha got married. Her sweet stay in heaven would end forever unless she found another such friend or, even better, a husband.

Lulu knew a certain matchmaker from the upper echelons of Saudi society that she had met at the salon. She had given the matchmaker countless free services at the salon in hopes of one day being granted priority in finding a suitable bachelor. Ensconced in the palace, Lulu dared to call the woman. She was delighted to find that the matchmaker had many eligible bachelors lined up for marriage. The only catch was that they wanted an equally glamorous bride of the same level, wealth, and family, deserving of their status. It simply was not fair to her. How could an average-looking girl from a middle-class family marry a billionaire or a prince? She wanted nothing less. It was easy for the rich and privileged, but it was one battle after another for the uninitiated to articulate their worth in front of these men. Was everything going to be a struggle for her?

Lulu continued to contemplate ways to enter the privileged circle. Even if it were a short engagement or marriage, it would offer her a way to raise the bar for future suitors as she would finally be a princess, or at the very least given a hefty sum of money and a house in her name that would secure her independence from her parents. Some of these profitable unions were arranged without the couple ever meeting in person beforehand and others with families present as chaperones. Sometimes the couple divorced soon after they wed, but the bride still kept the dowry, the status, and the title. Lulu regarded it as a no-lose situation.

Lulu spoke with several matchmakers who continued to insist that the rich only marry within their circle. Lulu proceeded unfazed, even when she was told that the aristocratic bachelors would appreciate only an educated, well-connected family and cultured bride. Good looks and a charming nature were a wonderful and welcome plus.

Unlike Sheikha, Lulu was neither tall nor slim; however, living in the palace had given her an inflated ego that led her to dress in overly tight clothes. The matchmakers repeatedly instructed her to lose weight, fix her style, and come back because a young woman like her would never work for the group of available bachelors. Lulu did not have time for this, so she simply took the clothes of Sheikha, because matching up clothes and styling them from a fashionable style vault was easier than picking and choosing on her own from a sea of clothes that in the end would look drab and everything but chic. Even then, the matchmakers would brush her off, until she had a better idea. She would simply say, "It's not for me, I am merely trying to find a suitor for my lady, *Lady Lulu*."

It was decided: She would use the face of Sheikha in place of her own until she snared herself someone worthy who would make her the queen of her castle. This sparked the flame of a plan to catapult Lulu into their realm—if not in a cat suit to meet her Batman, then at the very least as Lady Lulu to meet her Prince Charming. Sheikha would be her fairy godmother and her beneficiary all at once; only Sheikha need never know.

The plan was so easy to devise that it was almost a sin. Much too simple. All the tools were available for usage and exploitation. She began by using the photos she had saved of Sheikha—Sheikha with her horses and foals, Sheikha sketching, reading, being hugged by her father, with her pet dolphin, at her house in Monaco; Sheikha and her jewelry, her paintings, her luxury cars—the Maybach, the Rolls Royce, the Bentley—and, finally, Sheikha's exotic white tiger and his voracious appetite.

Lulu met with the matchmaker under the guise of representing a certain royal, or high-class lady of wealth, power, and beauty. No one could have handled the lady's public relations better than Lulu, and no one was better qualified for finding a match in that situation. She played the role of the lady's personal assistant perfectly, insisting that the lady's name remain a secret until the suitor spoke to her and that it would be for his ears alone. Lulu would select what "Lady Lulu" would approve of and would determine the best way forward for her. She would handle the introductions via telephone. BlackBerry chats would be the perfect medium for the inevitable exchange of images. She would take her time to properly welcome the suitor into her web. The wedding date would be set for three months from the first conversation, and it was to be absolutely non-negotiable.

Using Sheikha's picture and profile, the matchmaker soon found a suitor: a thirty-five-year-old Saudi royal, tall, dark and handsome, a Leo. He was a successful businessman, never married, and was thinking of settling down in the United States after the wedding because he had a portion of his investments in the United States and he enjoyed it there. Lulu's heart stopped. With luck like this, who needs black magic?

Catching the prince's attention was surprisingly easy. All she had to do was furnish him with a few select images of the alluring Sheikha as his potential bride-to-be. Human nature, curiosity, and vanity did the rest. The prince who was oh-so-hard to reach and discriminating was grateful for the introduction and begging for more.

Lulu had deliberately chosen someone who was not only a member of a royal family, but also was a business-man, ensuring that he would be away from home and too busy to actually insist on meeting often or soon. She let his liabilities be his own disadvantage in speaking to her as often as he would like. Too many inquiries could risk blow-ing her cover. Lulu remembered what her Aunt Khokha, who also worked in the salon, used to say: "You must be a tease with men. Once they have you, they lose interest. Without the chase there is no mystery and no reward, so why bother? Remember, it is best to be the apple at the end of the stick than to be the stick in their hand. The chase is the key." Thus, Lulu left little to no time before the actual wedding ceremony, when he would make her his wife and fall in love with her personality, at least. Even if he saw that she was not the beauty he was led to believe she was, she would compensate by being a loving partner. Otherwise, if all failed she would still keep the hefty dowry and she would live off the reputation that she was a prince's divorcee.

The prince was the only contact in the phone Lulu used, so none of her friends would know anything about it. She was careful to always leave him hungry for more, interrupting him as he was speaking or inquiring about her, promising him she would call him back—but of course she never did. To him she was unattainable, a mystery that left him more thirsty with every sip. She would read him a line that struck a deep chord within him, but then would say something absurd. When he would comment, she would say that she needed to call him back some other time or would just disconnect the call. The adrenaline rush was like that of a hunter pursuing prey that was unobtainable and impossible—and all the more intriguing.

Lulu saw no harm in using her friend, since it was for a good cause. Sheikha would understand that this would help Lulu to attain her goals in life: money, status, and a good-looking prince for a husband. She daydreamed about how she would join Sheikha and her husband in the future on their Swiss ski trips as lifelong friends.

Lulu carefully drew on the bank of images of Sheikha that she had saved, posting them at just the right point in a conversation with the prince. Lulu's real-life friends often told her she was a hilarious character, and she knew that her sense of humor was both her best asset and best chance at capturing the attention of her online prince. She was right: He was instantly interested. He searched for her. Constantly. Whenever he asked her a question that was too smart for her simple background, she would end the phone call, interrupting his thoughts and leaving the impression that she fully understood him. He was always left wondering, though he thought positively about her, as much as it would bother him. She seemed like she never had time for him, even though he was the one with a packed agenda.

The prince was particularly interested in the images of the horses and foals. Lulu was frightened of the large horses and being quite short, she found it difficult to mount a horse. Sheikha was five foot, seven inches tall and had been riding since she was three years old, with and without a saddle, so Lulu had many photographs of Lady Lulu on horseback. Unfamiliar with equine terminology, Lulu tried to joke her way through the prince's questions. He ignored the gaps in her knowledge of equine activities, perhaps because there was too much truth in the other things. Perhaps she wanted to avoid answering questions. Perhaps she was being coy. Lulu possessed details about the things Sheikha had done that only someone who had been there would know. For example, Sheikha sometimes let Lulu feed her horses, Snowdrop and Reeh Al Shemaal (North Wind), so she knew how to feed the horse with open fingers to avoid being bitten. She knew never to walk behind the horse, lest it kick in fright, and how horses sensed rain, earthquakes, and danger. Details like these kept the prince convinced and silent.

Lulu had to be careful with languages, however. She claimed that Lady Lulu had been educated abroad, like Sheikha, but Lulu's knowledge of English and French fell short of what one would expect from someone who had lived and studied in London and Paris. Indeed, her entire educational background was lacking, compared to the princess's. Some of the pictures she shared showed shelves packed with literary masterpieces, but Lulu did not know the difference between George Orwell and George Lucas. The prince would speak of the shabby-but-Boho Chic alleyways in Saint Germain, a gathering place for the educated and cultured, and she would say she hated poor corners and slums. Yet she also said she painted scenes on location in Paris, and a few of the paintings she had shared with him depicted the very same alleyways he mentioned. Odd indeed, and most queer. A curious nature, this intriguing and lovely Lady Lulu.

The images of Lady Lulu were always enticing, and they dissolved many a questioning thought. She was a royal like him, just as rich, traveled, cultured and educated, with a hunger to rediscover previously visited places with the same eagerness. Familiarity breeds approval. *How refreshing*, he thought to himself. The horses, the paintings, the beauty of her sad eyes, the romantic poetry, the alluring sound of her singing a short note, which he replayed several hundred times, and her beautiful, long hair were the net, and he, the fish.

The prince wanted to meet his bride before the wedding. He asked if he could fly in to see her, but she refused. She said it was her dream for him to see her in person on their wedding day, and for him to carry her away in a white carriage. His patience waned, and it began to look as if he would not be able to wait three months. When he insisted on seeing her, she explained that her father was very traditional and would expect the wedding to happen instantly and then introduce the bride. He understood that she was from a conservative family, but he was confident that there must be a way around it. She insisted otherwise.

The prince's suspicions began to grow. There was a little too much mystery surrounding Lady Lulu, especially the fact that she would not even reveal her father's name. Also, she said she spoke fluent Saudi Arabic because her best friend was Saudi. Hard to believe. The prince was a serious man and did not like women playing games with his heart, no matter how perfect she was. He told her he was coming to Kuwait for one day and expected to see her, even if it was in her father's house with a formal engagement. Fearing the whole scheme might fall apart, Lulu agreed, but she set the rules: She would only see him in a public place; her entourage would accompany her; they would not speak. The prince accepted the conditions, and Lulu set a date for the rendezvous.

Lulu called Sheikha and casually invited her to the Al Salhyia Mall to have lunch. The Fauchon Café in Al Salhyia is a famous spot for the old money in Kuwait, a place that people who are not fashionable or who are attempting to watch their weight should avoid.

Somewhere in the boisterous Fauchon Café sat the young prince. He immediately recognized Lady Lulu from the many pictures he had pored over for the last few months. He asked the maître d' to move him to another table, closer to the object of his affection. From his new vantage point, he filled his eyes to his content with his young princess.

She was everything she had said she was, and even more than she had shown him. There was a gentle grace that was impossible to sense in the hasty texts, and a serene glow of savoir-faire in the folding and unfolding of her napkin. The quiet movement of her slender hand requesting the menu, her bashful eyes and fan of lashes, the way her lips curved when she smiled warmed his heart and crowned the image he had of her in his mind. He pictured eating with her, her family and his family together, their children, their work and their travels. He wanted to apologize for his insist- ence and to compliment her, saying that it seemed the sun had come out to have lunch in Fauchon Café this day. He burned to join her.

He wanted to speak to her; after all, he *was* her fiancé, and he wanted to meet her family since he was in town. He was braver and more insistent and wanted to break the norms; he wanted to go introduce himself and sit down with her. It was the proper thing to do. She would definitely be delighted at his chivalry, and it would be a brilliant surprise. Who knew? He could be granted an audience with her while he lunched or maybe dine with the family with her present. His eyes did not belong to him anymore; they drank in her beauty as if they had never tasted anything like it before.

He texted her, but she never even looked at her BlackBerry. He did not understand. Unable to contain himself, he approached her to say hello, but she ignored him. He spoke to her, but she gave him a withering look and told him to leave her alone.

Feeling confused and a little insulted, he returned to his table. He toyed with his Caesar salad as she excused herself and walked past him toward the ladies' room. She was tall and slender, dressed in a light pink tweed Chanel jacket with a velvet border with gold and pearl buttons, and beige sailor trousers with similar gold buttons on either side. Her pearl earrings glimmered, and her straight, white teeth matched their opalescent gleam. With her hair gathered in a French twist, she looked like she had just walked out of a fashion magazine.

Accompanying her was a short, fat woman with exaggerated hips, tight jeans, and a bulging waistline. She was wearing chains and chains of long necklaces, silver eye shadow, and a long line of eyeliner that resembled the Egyptian pharaohs. No two friends together at the café could have looked more different or more odd. *The princess must have wanted to come in a hurry*, the prince thought, *and this was the only friend available. Clown looking, though.*

When the princess and her friend finished their meal and got up to leave, the prince threw more money than necessary on the table to pay his bill and followed them out the door. He remained at a distance as they proceeded to the car park. As the young women got into the princess's champagne-colored Porsche, the prince casually snapped a picture of the license plate as he walked by and said, "God bless you, my sweet."

When he got to his Range Rover, the prince texted the number plate to one of his contacts in the police department. As he waited to learn the family name of his beloved, he finally received a text from Lady Lulu. She apologized for her behavior, but said it was necessary since she could not let *her* entourage, Sheikha, know about him, as she was certain to tell her father and that could spoil all of their plans. She had mentioned that her family wanted to marry her off to her cousin but she wanted to know her husband-to-be beforehand. Hence the situation they were in right now.

The prince smiled to himself, thinking what an amazing moment it would be when her father spoke to her about him, all unannounced and unexpected and in full confidence that he was someone she would agree to marry because there was a pre-agreement and they were in love. He had forgotten his heart in the café, forgotten how to breathe like he used to. He looked at himself in the mirror and smiled. There was a delicate pleasure and joy in the corner of his eye and the curve of his smile when he caught his reflection.

The prince accepted the explanation of her indifferent behavior in public, but, after finding out her family name from her number plate, he decided to take matters into his own hands. Proceeding as a gentleman, he contacted her father, a respected sheikh, and asked to have coffee with him in the *majlis*.

After courteous greetings and some cordial chat, the prince stated his intentions. He wanted to marry Princess Lulu. Her father looked confused. He had only one daughter of marriageable age, and she was already engaged. The prince could not believe what he was hearing.

"Princess Lulu is engaged?" the prince asked in amazement.

"My daughter most assuredly is," said Sheikha's father. "But that's another thing: Her name is Sheikha, not Lulu. She has a friend named Lulu, a Saudi girl who lives in our care. She is my daughter's entourage as she has failed in university but she is the daughter of a hairdresser, not a head of state."

Sheikha's father laughed at his own wordplay.

The prince smiled, more in embarrassment than in amusement, thinking to himself that his love had a sharper wit than her father did.

Sheikha's father explained that Lulu was like his daughter, but he still deemed it best to propose to her through her own father.

"Her father is in Riyadh," Sheikha's father said. "He sells camels, I think."

The prince was a businessman and royal with many years of experience in public attacks, scandals and swindles, but this was new to him. Hurt and angry, he seethed in Kuwait for a day trying to clear his thoughts on how to proceed. Lady Lulu texted him, but he ignored all of her attempts at contact. She asked him if he did not like how she looked when he saw her. She explained how she had to act detached because everything is watched carefully by the socially active and camera-happy people in Kuwait. She was afraid of her reputation being tarnished had she shown her true affections and excited reaction to meeting him. Being caught on camera talking to a stranger and publicly entertaining him is not a comfortable situation for a woman to be put in, especially at such a sensitive and marriage-ripe age.

Her lies and excuses only made the prince angrier, but he held his tongue. He burned, tearing himself up inside at how stupid he had been. He felt gullible, naïve, and taken for a fool. What did this camel herder's daughter want? To trick him into marrying her and then give him a heart attack when he entered to meet his bride, only to find that she was a fake? They say life is a tragic comedy, but he was in so much pain at being deceived that he could only feel the horror of a broken heart, the disappointment, and the sweet-tasting lies poisoning him. What kind of sadistic joke was this?

As he waited for his flight to leave Kuwait, the prince decided to call the number his police contact had given to him, not the number Lady Lulu used to send him messages.

After rehearsing what he would say a hundred times in his head, the prince pressed the "call" button.

Sheikha answered. The princess had only spoken a few words to him at Fauchon Café, and they were abrupt and serious, but the prince instantly recognized the voice of his muse. It matched the seven-second voice message of her singing and began melting the ice that had frosted his heart. Her voice was warm and kind; he had not counted on that. He wanted to introduce himself and then tell her that he knew that she was engaged and soon to be married, that he respected that, but he wanted to speak to her for clarification of a situation. He wanted, needed, and demanded closure. Otherwise, it would burn him to his dying days. It was his right.

"*Salam alikum,*" he said, and then hesitated, forgetting his orchestrated lines. The anger bubbled inside of him.

"*Aliakum asalam,*" Sheikha responded quietly and collectedly.

"Lu- Sheikha?" All he could feel was a knot in his throat. He was drowning in doubt and was confused. What was supposed to be a romantic rendezvous had turned out to be a nightmare from which he could not awaken. Not only was this a scam, but he was trapped, because he had strong feelings for a person who did exist, but who did not even know he did.

"I am Prince Sultan," he said, drawing out his family name. He paused. "I hardly know where to begin."

"Why not begin at the beginning?" said Sheikha. She was expecting it to be someone asking for an interview or

49

financial support, or possibly a friend's relative who was in town, inquiring after something in Kuwait, and she would look into how to help him.

"Perhaps it's better to begin at the end," Prince Sultan replied. "I spoke to your father to propose marriage to you, only to find out that I have been taken for a ride." His voice was calm but strained, like a trembling volcano slowly waking and collecting momentum.

"My father mentioned that someone wanted to propose to me, or to Lulu," said Sheikha. An awkward silence followed. "I'm married; umm, I will be in a month anyway."

More silence.

"Lulu lied to me," said the prince at last. "I was going to marry you. Even with this crazy idea of only speaking to you, and meeting you only on the wedding day. I loved you—I loved a lie. She used you. Did you know about it? Do you do this often? Have you no shame? I'm very angry. I'm not a toy! How dare you!"

Prince Sultan realized his eyes were welling up and his raised blood pressure caused a vein in his forehead to beat harder, becoming visible in his anger. He swallowed his ire, tears, and words. Waiting for an answer, he sat in silence looking down, with his head in his hands and the headset comfortably set in his ears. He could feel the perspiration on his forehead.

Sheikha was embarrassed that a prince from a foreign country had proposed to her when she was engaged to be married soon. How awkward. She also was frightened, because he sounded angry and she dared not ask him what was going on. She could hear the brokenheartedness in his deep voice, and she was curious as to what had led him on. She had her suspicions, but she did not voice them.

"I'm sorry, but I don't know what you're talking about," said Sheikha. She dared not discuss with him what happened. Clearly he felt insulted, and she feared provoking him further.

"Princess, I know everything about you—your likes, your dislikes, where you have traveled, the animals you raised, your hopes, your dreams, your sense of humor. I fell in love with you, even though we had never met. I proposed only to find out that you are not even available."

If bitterness and disappointment had a musical note, she could hear it in his trailing voice.

It was a defeated voice now, bitter and choked with rage. He had not intended to say any of that, but his heart was breaking. It was not fair to have so much feeling for someone and for that person to be completely unaware of what even the sound her voice did to his quaking heart. This must be what they called one-sided love, and the worst part was that she did not even know he existed. She did not even know who exactly he was. There were thousands of royals, and no one deserved to be tricked like that. It was shameful being a part of this fiasco, even if only as an audience, because of the risk of being thought to be an accomplice.

Sheikha was beginning to get worried. With her wedding preparations already underway, she did not need a scandal at this time. She thought someone had proposed to her as a joke because her wedding was in a month. Or that it was actually sweet that someone had proposed to her friend Lulu, thinking that she was her sister. "Prince Sultan, I'm afraid I don't know what you're talking about," she said. "My apologies, but please explain what I've done and what I can do to rectify or make amends. I'm deeply sorry for the muddle-up, but I had no idea whatsoever that this was happening under my roof." Her tone was firm, but she was trembling and hoped that she could explain that she was innocent. "I have been busy with my master's thesis, work, and family."

"I know your schedule, where you go and what you do—your application and bugs, your horses, your family, and this was all a lie." He interrupted himself and then trailed off as if he were thinking and reminiscing.

"It was your friend Lulu," said the prince. "She took your identity and almost tricked me into marrying her. What kind of sick, demented people do you keep in your entourage as your hairdressers or friends?"

He needed to head to the plane as it was taking off, so he began walking toward the boarding gate. He revealed everything that he had been told and shown: her pictures, writing, poetry, travel, animals, and lifestyle.

"Why do you have a daughter of a camel herder escorting you?" he blurted out.

"I swear, I didn't know," trembled Sheikha. "I'm in love with my fiancé and I'm very happy with him. I had no idea about any of this. Lulu is sometimes impulsive, but I did not expect that she would do anything like this. This is beyond absurd!"

Her voice trailed off. The prince could not hear her nervousness; she seemed serene and almost amused, but he needed to voice his pain, otherwise he would die, drowning in his sea of misery. In a rage that eventually cooled, he told her he met "Lady Lulu" through a persistent matchmaker who promised him a dream wife who would be the love of his life. He thought since matchmaking was commonly done in the region, why not give it a try? He was single, and his mother had been nagging him to settle down with a woman she would approve of. She was at a late stage of cancer, and he promised her that he would entertain the first suitable bride, if any. He warmed to the idea when he saw Sheikha's picture and heard her details. His communication with her was via texts, emails, online chats and the images of her and her life that were sent. He was caught in a net that entangled him more and more every day. Now he was angry at the wasted time and feelings, the insult to his name, and the humiliation of having to involve another royal in this mess. He left in the middle of convention week in the States with several entertaining speakers and many opportunities to discuss business yet to come because he thought he heard his heart calling. He was a straight shooter and wanted to understand better what he had gotten himself into. He apologized again, but felt that he was apologizing to his own feelings. When were they going to invent a painkiller for heartbreak?

Sheikha held back from saying how betrayed she felt but could not stop telling the prince how sorry she was for having been used as the bait, pawn, and carrot in a cruel game. She was ashamed of this ugly action by her friend. She admitted that it would have been an injustice for her to allow this debacle if she had known about it, but swore that she had nothing to do with it. She had heard Lulu speak with bright eyes about women who were given wealth, a title, and a house when they divorced but had dismissed it as silly talk. As she thought back, she remembered Lulu had remarked how it was done all the time and how normal it was. She was sorry she had not heeded the drums of war. The simple girl had devised a strategic plan to achieve her status with no thought of how it might go wrong or who it might injure.

The prince was hurt, disappointed, and insulted; Sheikha could hear it, but acknowledging it further would border on concern that could be misunderstood as affection and tenderness, and she already was red in the face from embarrassment. She was firm but polite, apologizing and praying this would end quietly.

Prince Sultan expressed how much he had enjoyed hearing about her life. He stopped short of telling her how much he would miss her news. He had fallen in love with a spirit, and, as distorted as it was, could not dissolve the attachment to it. His ice was thawing, and his heart was warming. It had been the shortest and sweetest intimacy he had known in his life.

As he closed the phone and fastened his seatbelt, the prince had tears in his eyes. He wished he could have a cigarette to calm his nerves. He had deliberately put the call off until the last minute because he did not know what to say or how to say it. As the plane took off, all he could think about was the images he had pictured while he sat opposite his love at the café. Now he regretted that he could not call Sheikha again, for everything that he wanted to say was said; however, there were things he needed to hear that he could not get closure on now. The call he made to vent his anger had come full circle, completing the perfect image of the independent and beautiful woman he had wanted to have standing beside him for tomorrow and for the rest of his life. He had been so happy, but now he sank to a deep level of sadness. To realize exactly what you have lost before you ever possessed it is a tragedy.

Before the call from Prince Sultan, Sheikha had been walking on clouds. She was soon to be married. Already her trousseau exceeded any girl's dreams—a cavalcade of iconic, silk-wrapped boxes: blue from Tiffany, red from Cartier, brown from Louis Vuitton, silver from Chaumet, and navy from Graff; all delivered in a train of luggage from Goyard and Hermès. The excitement had made her lose touch with reality. Reality struck when the prince told her that Lulu, the Saudi student who had moved in with her family, had used Sheikha's pictures, interests, and even voicemail message to lure him into an engagement. All this was overwhelming and emotionally draining.

Sheikha felt partly to blame for the fiasco with the prince. Preoccupied with the preparations for her marriage, she had largely ignored Lulu for almost a year. They had stopped going out together and spoke at home only when they met by chance. Not that Lulu seemed to mind. Once she failed in school, she simply stayed at home, treating the palace as a well-appointed, free hotel, coming and going with little or no attachment to Sheikha or her family. When finally asked to leave, Lulu would cry and say she felt more at home and loved than she did in Saudi Arabia and would promise to study harder and succeed, because she did not want to return to her home country. Sheikha realized that if she had been closer to Lulu, her friend might not have concocted her crazy plan, or, if she did, she might have discovered it. Regardless, the time had come for a quick, clean break.

Sheikha confronted Lulu and asked her to leave. Lulu was in tears. She said she did not mean to hurt Sheikha. All she had wanted was a bridge to reach her secure home, and she sincerely believed the prince would have loved her eventually—it happened, or at least it *could* happen. She only needed an opportunity to marry her prince. Simple. *Only* an introduction. The end justified the means, did it not? And everyone would end up happy. She felt she had earned the right to borrow her friend's character, face, status and all else if the character, face and status she wanted to be with in order to be happy required this entrance. Pure Machiavellianism at its best. After all, was Machiavelli's book not called *The Prince*?

Lulu apologized to Sheikha for stealing her identity but stubbornly clung to her justification for her behavior. Everyone, she said, would have been happy in the end. Sheikha smiled at the thought of Prince Sultan being happy with Lulu as his bride. A few minutes over the phone with him were enough to know that Lulu was everything he would not have wanted in a woman. *No sense arguing*, Sheikha thought, and, although it broke her heart to be so cold to someone she once loved, she told Lulu she was no longer welcome in her home. Lulu was to collect her travel documents and belongings and leave immediately and quietly. The family need not know of her fiasco. Sheikha, who had already scheduled a flight to Paris, would pay for Lulu's flight back to Saudi Arabia. When she returned from Paris, Lulu needed to be gone.

The night before Sheikha's flight, Lulu stood outside her door and begged to speak with her again. Sheikha had locked the door to her bedroom and welded closed the door to her heart. Her fiancé spoke to her that night and she told him that Lulu was leaving. He had never liked Lulu and was pleased, especially since he had thought Sheikha was feeling sad at having to soon leave her family and her friend behind. Lulu had betrayed her in ways no one ever had before, embarrassing her in front of another royal and country. Sheikha never wanted to see or even think of her again. As Lulu whined and cried outside her door, Sheikha deleted and blocked her from WhatsApp, Facebook, Instagram, Viber, and Twitter.

Sheikha left for Paris early the next morning, while Lulu was still in bed. At the airport, she again recalled the phone conversation with the prince. When the plane lifted off, Sheikha relaxed for the first time since the prince's call. At last her worries were behind her.

Sheikha made the rounds of her favorite designers in Paris and London, choosing a few select items of the latest designer wear to complete her dream trousseau. She and her groom would be going on an extended honeymoon, and she needed the wardrobe of a young married woman, not one of a single woman. The difference was subtle, but she knew her new husband would notice and approve.

On the flight back to Kuwait, Sheikha thought about what drove Lulu to try to trick Prince Sultan into marriage. She could not understand how desperate Lulu was to marry into royalty, how the demons racked her mind—a kind of insanity. She decided that Lulu suffered from a severe inferiority complex, having been brought up in highly conservative Saudi society, with the added stigma of being the offspring of a "man thief." She had moved away to a place where open-minded individuals valued her for who she was, rather than for what she was. In Sheikha she had found an affluent but genuine friend whose chauffeur-driven cars and personal attendants were at her beck and call. She had finally found the warmth of a home that she had always yearned for in Riyadh. She would often visit Sheikha's grandmother, since she never had the opportunity to have interacted with her own and she basked in the affection showered upon her by an elderly maternal figure. She attended weddings and birthday parties with Sheikha and her sisters and shared in all the family celebrations. She was taught to drive—which was not allowed in her homeland—and then enrolled in a driving school and got her driver's license. She was allowed the privilege of driving any car in the garage her heart desired. She even enjoyed the family's weekend dune dueling in the deserts. In short, Sheikha's loving family treated her as one of the daughters. Lulu had borrowed a royal lifestyle, so she did not consider it wrong to borrow a royal identity.

Sheikha had just graduated from university and enrolled in a Master's program in the evening, since she worked full time at the IT company. Her entire day was spent working, commuting, and chatting on the phone with her fiancé. She would retire to bed by 10:30 pm with hardly any time left for Lulu. Lulu would go out with her newfound friends and come back with tales of amazement and adventure. Sheikha regarded her as a younger sister and tried to shield her from the hidden dangers that young women sometimes end up exposing themselves to. Sheikha still found it hard to believe that her many acts of kindness had been rewarded with Lulu's betrayal of confidence.

Sheikha's chauffeur met her at the airport, and everything appeared normal as they entered the compound. Sheikha went inside and the chauffeur followed with her luggage. Cherryl and Generose, the family's maids, greeted Sheikha and started to take her luggage upstairs.

"Unpack the trunk in Lulu's old room," said Sheikha. "I want to use it as a fitting room."

"But Mam, Lulu is still here," said Generose.

"What?" asked Sheikha.

"There was a problem with her passport," Cherryl explained.

"Fine. Put everything in my room."

Sheikha greeted her mother and answered a few questions about her trip before going upstairs. Generose was in her bedroom, hanging her new clothes in her closet, which was otherwise empty.

"Where are my things?" asked Sheikha.

"Madam?"

"Where are my clothes? What did you do with them?"

"I did not do anything, Madam. The closet was empty, so I hung the clothes here."

"But why is the closet empty? Who took the clothes?"

"I don't know, Madam."

Sheikha noticed something amiss on her vanity as well. "Did someone clear off my vanity?" she asked.

"I don't think so, Madam. Cherryl and I only cleaned as usual."

"Where are my perfumes? My products?"

"Madam, I'm sorry but I do not know where they are."

"Has someone been here? Has someone been in my room?"

"No one except for me and Cherryl."

"Then where is everything?"

Sheikha did not wait for an answer. She stormed into Lulu's room. Her unwelcome house guest was lying on the bed, reading a magazine.

"Where are my things?"

"What?" asked Lulu.

Sheikha walked to a closet and threw it open. It was stuffed with Lulu's clothes. Sheikha spun around.

"Where are my things?" Sheikha shouted.

Lulu laid down the magazine, annoyed. "Why are you yelling at me?" she said.

"Lulu, where are the items from my trousseau? And my perfumes? My personal products? And who knows what else?"

"How should I know? I'm not your maid," Lulu snapped. "Some of my things are missing as well. I thought you had the maids pack them for me."

"Are you insane?" screamed Sheikha. She hurried out the door and down the stairs. "Mother, where are my things?"

"What are you shouting about, dear?" asked her mother.

"Mother, my closets are empty, my bags are missing, my dresses are not in the closet, and my shoe rack is bare!"

"That's ridiculous."

"Of course it's ridiculous. Completely ridiculous. But it's true. Everything from basic necessities to finest luxuries is gone."

"Impossible," said her mother.

"Wait, wait, wait. Where is that kid brother of mine?"

"Khalid went to the mall with his friends."

"That little prankster. He did this. Too bad he was not here to see my reaction."

"I don't think . . ."

Sheikha cut off her mother. "It had to be him. Who else could it be? What a relief. There for a moment I was scared. Of course he has hidden everything."

"I don't think he would do something like that," said Sheikha's mother.

"You don't think, but he did. Things don't just get up and walk out on their own. Call me the minute he is home."

Sheikha went back to her room just as Generose was finishing up.

"Did Khalid take my things?" Sheikha asked.

"I didn't see anything, Madam. I would have told you, Madam. I know you are upset."

"Of course, Generose. Thank you. Please send Cherryl up with a sparkling water."

Sheikha sat down at her empty vanity. She looked at herself in the mirror and choked back tears. How could her brother do this to her? Yes, he was young, but he should have known better than to give someone a fright right before her wedding. It was those stupid television shows he watched, always getting a laugh from someone's misfortune. It was amazing he did not shoot a video of her reaction to post on YouTube.

That was when it hit her.

It was not Khalid. He would have been there to film her reaction. She looked around the room as a shiver shook her delicate frame. Someone had been there. A thief.

What else had he taken?

She pulled open a drawer of the vanity. Empty. Even her brush and hair dryer were missing.

Sheikha felt nauseous. Who would take her personal effects, except for someone desperate to ruin her life and wedding? How could the other things of clear and evident value remain untouched, but only she—the bride—was ransacked?

She called the police without a second thought.

"I want to report a burglary," she said.

When she revealed her identity to the police, they immediately sent a captain to the villa.

"What is all this?" said Sheikha's father when the police officer arrived.

"All of my things have been stolen, Father," said Sheikha. "My entire trousseau. Everything, except for what I brought back from this trip."

Her father sat in as the police officer interviewed Sheikha. As she began to list what was missing, the officer stopped her.

"Perhaps you can email the complete list," he said, handing her his card. "I assume these things are truly missing and not somewhere on the premises."

"No, at first I thought it was my brother playing a trick on me, but it was not."

"And have you interrogated your domestic help?"

"That will not be necessary," said Sheikha's father. "They have been with us since before Sheikha was born. They would not take a bite of food without asking us first, I can assure you."

"I did ask them," said Sheikha. "It wasn't them."

"We have this houseguest," said Sheikha's father, "a friend of Sheikha's. Lulu. A college drop-out. We recently asked her to leave our home. Perhaps this is her revenge."

"I asked Lulu, too," interrupted Sheikha. "And I searched her room. It wasn't her. There's nothing there. Besides, who would bite the hand that feeds them?"

"I see," said the officer. He turned to Sheikha's father.

"Sir, I would like to take this Lulu in for questioning. She had intimate knowledge of the house, your daughter's belongings, and your daughter's whereabouts when they went missing. Perhaps she knows more than she is telling. The pressure of the police station has a way of drawing out the truth."

Sheikha's father agreed. He called Cherryl and asked her to bring Lulu downstairs, dressed and ready to leave. Sheikha excused herself and went to the family room, where her mother sat, reading. She did not want to see Lulu before she left. It was almost embarrassing and deep down inside she did not want to believe that her friend, whom she had housed for two years, would be capable of such a deed.

What the officer said made sense. It seemed likely that it was someone in the household. Cherryl and Generose, the immediate maids designated to Sheikha's and Lulu's care, were questioned, albeit undoubtedly innocent. But information fragments would make the picture clearer and bring them closer to solving the puzzle. Khalid, too, was innocent. It seemed like it had to be Lulu, but Sheikha was not sure about anything anymore.

Lulu left with the police officer, and the police kept her overnight. She came back at noon the next day, bright-eyed and excited, full of stories of how polite the police officers were to her. Over lunch, she told Sheikha and Khalid how the police repeated the same questions many times, but to no effect. She said every time they began getting difficult, she would sternly remind them to be respectful, claiming her father was an advisor to the King of Saudi Arabia and like an uncle to him. The police were taken aback by her confidence and heeded caution in questioning her. At last she was free to go, feeling like a victorious gladiator. She returned to the palace and ate her lunch heartily, with a full appetite and not a care in the world.

With Lulu exonerated, Sheikha began to worry that a professional burglar had targeted her family. Fearing her jewels would be next on the list of robberies, she decided to transfer everything to the bank. She opened her safe and put everything into a jewelry case. She held a bracelet across her hand and thought she should have everything cleaned before she put it in the bank. That way it would be ready for her wedding day. As she placed the last of the jewelry in the case, Lulu walked in.

"Your father wants to see you," she said. "The police officer is back and he wants to interview you again."

A look of triumph gleamed in Lulu's eyes.

"All right. Thanks," said Sheikha.

Lulu stood at the door for a moment, but Sheikha did not move. "I will be right down," she said.

Sheikha thought about putting everything back in the safe, but she did not want to keep the officer waiting. She slipped the case into a thick paper bag and placed it on the shelf in her closet.

The officer had come by to see if Sheikha or her father had thought of anyone else who might have had access to the home.

Generose arrived with tea and dates for the officer, Sheikha, and her father.

"What is your assessment, then?" asked Sheikha's father.

"Very hard to say," said the officer, taking a sip of tea. "Without surveillance cameras or an eyewitness, I cannot rule out a professional job. I am afraid we have seen this before: professional thieves targeting the royal family, but usually it involves a trusted maid, friend or person from the household even."

"That has been happening since the Middle Ages," said Sheikha's father.

"Yes, but today's thieves have telephoto lenses and night-vision goggles to watch your comings and goings, all-terrain vehicles to approach your palace from the open desert, and they can track your location through your social media—Instagram, Facebook, Viber, WhatsApp."

Sheikha's father glanced at his daughter.

"I take it you posted to social media while you were gone," said the officer.

Sheikha nodded.

"They knew you were gone," he said. "You would be amazed at what we have seen. Sometimes thieves plant audio bugs and even spy cams in a home to track the family's movements."

The idea of a spy camera anywhere near her bedroom made Sheikha shudder.

"How do they get inside to plant these devices?" Sheikha's father asked.

"Sometimes they have accomplices who work in home services—electricians, plumbers, even people who install televisions. That kind of thing. Often they recruit someone who works for the family."

"I told you, our servants have been with us for decades," said Sheikha's father. "If they would steal they would not steal clothes that don't fit them, and most certainly they would not steal their mistress's wedding gown and then remain in the house to be caught red-handed."

"Understood," said the police captain. "But never underestimate the power of greed."

"I would trust them with my life," said Sheikha's father, raising his voice. "I dismissed my nurses, trusting these maids to bring me my heart and blood pressure medication."

"Of course," said the officer. "I did not mean to implicate your staff. Now if these thieves are professionals, chances are they will strike another palace. They will not stop if they got away with it once. God willing, we will catch them next time and they will still have your things."

"God willing," said Sheikha.

The officer asked a few more questions over tea and then left. Sheikha hurried upstairs to get her jewelry so she could drop it off at the jeweler's before it closed. The chauffeur walked her into the shop for security. When Sheikha opened the box for the jeweler, she found to her horror that it was empty. She instantly called Lulu on her mobile, but she did not answer. The chauffeur drove Sheikha back home as she called Lulu's number again and again. There was no answer. When they got home, Lulu was gone.

Sheikha still found it hard to believe that Lulu could do such a thing. Yet it seemed clear that the culprit could be no other, and so she had no choice but to call the police again. As she waited for the captain to arrive, she received a text from Lulu: *I love you, Sheikha. You are all my family and more. It hurt me that you would think that I would bite the hand that fed me. You gave me a roof when I was a lost stranger here. Why would I ever want to hurt you?*

Sheikha still did not want to believe that someone she had once loved could hurt her so much. She texted Lulu back: *Please return my things and there will be no scandal.*

Lulu did not answer.

"What evidence do you have that she took your jewels?" asked the officer when he arrived.

"She saw I had taken them out of the safe and was putting them in the jewelry box, and now she is gone, and the jewels are gone. She must have gone through my room while we were down here discussing the case."

"Do you have a picture of her?"

Sheikha sent a photo of Lulu to the police officer's phone.

"We will pick her up," said the captain. "Do you know where she might have gone?"

"I have no idea."

"If you hear from her or think of anything else, let us know."

A couple days later, the secretary employed by Sheikha's family called Sheikha. Lulu had left her passport with him for visa renewal, and she had called to see if it was ready. The secretary informed her that it was not and, having heard about the theft of Sheikha's belongings, called Sheikha immediately.

"Do not give her the passport, give it to the police so she will walk into her own judgment," instructed Sheikha.

A couple days later, Sheikha was shocked to receive this message from Lulu: *Honey, your only problem is that you have no proof. If I don't get my passport, I will ask my father to do what's necessary to get it from you.*

Gone was the shy Saudi girl, and out came a monster. Sheikha notified the police of the new message and mentioned that her family had Lulu's passport. That gave the captain an idea. He suggested that they lure Lulu to the secretary's office by saying the passport was ready. The police would be there to apprehend her.

The plan worked. Lulu came to collect her travel documents and the police arrested her. This time, they were not so kind and patient. They locked her in a cell with several criminals. It did not matter. Lulu told them nothing. She was just as wild as the criminals she was locked in with and would fight verbally and physically like a stray cat. They searched the room where she was staying, but did not find anything of Sheikha's. Without more evidence, the police would have to let her go.

Sheikha had just twenty days to her wedding. She had no clothes, wedding gown, jewels, hair accessories, shoes, or underwear. Her phones, iPads, and credit cards were gone, as were personal items like her toothbrush, toothpaste, and bathroom slippers. A typical robber would take money and jewelry, but this one also had taken her hairbrushes, shampoos, eye drops, contact lenses, and sunglasses. Every day Sheikha woke up to find that something else was missing.

Each time Sheikha discovered something was gone, she updated her list for the police. One of these updates broke the case open. Sheikha remembered that she had purchased a Vertu mobile phone but had never used it. When she took the box out of a drawer, it felt unusually light. When she opened it, the phone was missing. She stood looking at the empty box for a moment and had a dim recollection of saving the number in her phone. She immediately checked, and it was there. She called the police with a description of the phone and the number. It was a thrill, as this was the first clue that might be traceable.

The police found that the stolen phone had been used to call three numbers: two in Kuwait and one in the Yemen. The numbers pointed to two Egyptians—one working in Zain Telecommunications and the other in a local driving school—and a Yemeni in Yemen working in a cargo company. The Egyptian men were brought to police headquarters. One of the Egyptians was released, as he appeared only to have received the stolen phone for his brother, the driving instructor. The driving instructor told the police he had done nothing other than receive a suitcase from a young woman, which, in his fright, he brought to police. It was his cut of the deal, and the police promised him they would go easy on him if he would admit to all the crime details and help clear the case as soon as possible. He tried to play the gullible fool, saying he had been tricked into taking the goods as payment for helping the woman send a few suitcases to his friend in Yemen. According to the Egyptian, the Yemeni was instructed to store the pieces until further notice. Under pressure from the police, the driving instructor gave up the woman's name and pointed her out from behind a glass when they brought her to the headquarters.

It was Lulu.

The Egyptian had recommended that Lulu send her items to Egypt, but the goat herder's daughter thought it would cost too much since Egypt levies a tax on the entry of large quantities of goods. She did not want to pay the taxes, or risk having her cover blown. She decided to send the suitcases to a friend in Yemen, who would then forward the stolen goods to Riyadh, where Lulu would sell them in her mother's salon. Nothing would be traceable to her. She could leave Sheikha's house, have her luggage searched at the airport or even upon arrival in Saudi Arabia, and no one would find proof that she had done anything. Did they not say you are innocent until proven guilty? She thought that by giving the Egyptian the new phone she found among Sheikha's things to make the arrangements, nothing could be traced. She was wrong.

The police contacted the Yemeni, who returned items out of fear of being arrested. Every thief had taken a rather large suitcase and selected what he would like from the batch. The bags arrived at Sheikha's palace amidst celebration. The elation did not last long. The first suitcase contained Sheikha's wedding gown, or what was left of it. It was torn, snipped, and burned, and had muddy shoe prints on it. The delicate silk embroidery and crystals had been crushed. The dress was ruined. There is no wedding when there is no gown.

Over the next few weeks, the police returned to the palace again and again with broken pieces of Sheikha's life. Her wedding was ruined, and half of her jewelry had been sold in Saudi Arabia, Yemen, and the United Arab Emirates, and could not be recovered.

Every day, Lulu sent Sheikha messages and apologies, but friendship is like a porcelain cup, precious and rare: Once broken, it can be mended, but a crack will always be there.

The police threatened Lulu with life imprisonment in a high security prison if she did not return a Piaget watch worth $150,000. Naturally, she led the police to the watch's new owner, who had paid only $2,000 for it on the black market. Lulu had sold the watch when Sheikha was still unaware that friendships have expiry dates, and that jealousy twists even iron ore in its wrath of fire.

Lulu's parents came to Sheikha's family's palace and begged to have their daughter released. They promised to return any stolen goods or to pay the difference. Generous and forgiving, Sheikha's family arranged Lulu's release. After she and her family left to Saudi Arabia, they disappeared.

Lulu studied makeup art. She dazzled her customers and, with the coming of Instagram, rose to stardom. As her reputation grew, she instructed the Moroccans who knew her to call her Sultana Lulu, after the blockbuster Turkish historical soap opera, *Hareem Al Sultan* (The Women of the Sultan). Afraid of having to pay the debt that she was guilty of, she went to another matchmaker and paid her in makeup and salon services to find a new suitor. The matchmaker brought her an older man. His wealth was small, but his cousin was married to a powerful judge who they thought could pull a few strings on Lulu's behalf. Lulu married her suitor within a few weeks. He paid a dowry of only 100,000 Saudi riyals, leaving the matchmaker furious because neither Lulu nor her husband had the decency to pay her customary fee.

Despite Lulu's hope that her ordeal was over, her crimes would not simply go away. A lawyer for Sheikha's family contacted her new husband, demanding payment. When her husband asked Lulu about it, she denied everything. Her husband was furious and understood from his wife that it was all a lie made up against her. He said the lawyer was slandering his wife. Lulu should have told her husband the truth. Instead, when her partners in crime came clean, she was ordered to pay restitution.

It was a debacle, especially since she was married to someone from the judicial system who had a duty to represent all that was just and true and yet ended up defending a common thief. She embarrassed an entire nation in front of another royal who did nothing but show her kindness.

She continues to make payments to her former friend's bank account today.

I Will Never Leave You

O NE WOULD THINK THAT breaking up with a bad boyfriend would be the end of the nightmare, but that is not always the case. My worst nightmare began after I broke up with my fiancé, whom I had known since high school.

I was studying multimedia at the American University in Dubai and had been engaged to a doctor completing his residency in a local hospital. He worked long hours and had plans to further pursue his studies abroad. When we discussed our future, he made it clear that he did not want me to distract him by possibly having children. His plan was to leave me behind in the Emirates and visit whenever possible, depending on his workload in the United States, Germany or wherever he was accepted to study and work. We politely and amicably ended it, because I did not feel I was a priority in his career-driven life and was worried I would be emotionally starved over the long term.

During Eid, I received a welcome phone call from my old friend, crush, and high school heartthrob Hamdan, who was studying in Boston, Massachusetts.

"Happy Eid, Sawsan," he said. "I heard you are graduating before me and that you broke up with your fiancé."

Silence followed and we both laughed. I was happy to hear from an old friend I had truly missed.

"I'm glad you broke up," he continued, "because I wanted to tell you something: The truth is I've always been in love with you. I wanted to propose to you, but you got engaged before I graduated. I had given up all hope, but then I heard your engagement is off. So before I'm too late again, I'd like to get a hold of you before someone else proposes. Will you marry me, Sawsan?"

It happened so fast that for a moment I thought he was joking. The silence that followed insinuated that he was serious. I think he expected me to digest this and respond within moments, but I was flabbergasted and lost for words.

The phone call was too early in the morning and was too much of an answered prayer to be true. It was too sudden and intense, and I was in the hospital recovering from a serious car accident, trying to use my drugged senses to understand it all. Here was the coolest, funniest, and tallest person I knew, proposing to me. I was speechless. Gone were the carefully rehearsed responses in front of the dressing room mirror to such a perfectly sweet request. There was no introduction, and no need for it. I automatically said "yes," and was left feeling numb. I casually forgot to ask for my parents' permission and felt completely giddy.

In those early days of our engagement, he spoke about how he had always known that I was the one destined to be his wife, the mother of his children, and his friend for life. Nothing on earth could have been better than those sweet moments shared between blooming hearts in the spring of their youth. I was sleeping on clouds, walking on air, and picking daisies whenever he called, sent me a text message or brought me flowers, chocolates, or gifts.

Hamdan asked my father for my hand in marriage. My parents were a little surprised at the sudden news, especially so soon after I had ended another engagement, but they were delighted for me because everyone knew I had always been obsessed with him. My sisters and friends were thrilled, and we began to discuss the preparations for the wedding. We set the date of the wedding for one year from the engagement, when both of us would have graduated. We called it our graduation and wedding dinner ball. I do not remember ever having felt quite so ecstatically happy before.

Trouble began the first week of our engagement. Hamdan would ask to speak with me all the time. I thought it was sweet that he was so attached. I thought that was what I wanted, was it not? In my still-adolescent mind, I related his exaggerated attachment to how much he truly cared about me. At night he did not want to put the phone down; he sheepishly asked if he could stay on the phone even after I fell asleep. He wanted to hear me breathing as I slept. He said he simply could not wait for me to be by his side, sharing a bed. He asked to stay on the phone, headset, and speakerphone with me all day and night—as much as fourteen hours a day, ignoring all other calls.

After the first week, the novelty wore off; his requests and fixation on me became annoying. He began to ask if he could stay with me twenty-four hours a day, even in classes, during discussions with my friends, and when I was doing my homework. The attachment was turning into obsessive-compulsive behavior, and I was not feeling comfortable with the changes in my fiancé. He was not the same happy-go-lucky and witty gentleman who had captured the attention of every girl with his smile, his charm, and his chivalry. He had turned into a nuisance.

He began to get angry at small things and his outbursts pushed us apart for short periods. He would get upset even when my phone battery died and we had to spend a few hours out of touch. Often I came home to find my parents sitting in the living room, quietly discussing how Hamdan had called them after he had just come off the phone with me, inquiring after my safety and well-being. It amused them, but it exasperated me.

His ridiculous behavior was spiraling out of control, and, besides overwhelming me, it also made me question my reasons for wanting to be with him. His demands were stressing the relationship before the ship had set sail. I began to think I did not know him at all. Being friends is very different from being lovers and spouses. The type of relationship changes the expectations of treatment. A man who wishes to be a business partner or a friend will not make as many demands, but if he were to view himself as a lover or partner in marriage he might ask for more control—sometimes more than would be humanly possible, asphyxiating a healthy relationship even in its early stages. That was exactly what was happening to me.

Entertaining Hamdan's neediness was exhausting me, so, naturally, I spoke to him about his overprotective nature. That is when his angry trait appeared—an irritation that would erupt with a force I had never seen before. It would end up with this big man demanding my full cooperation and questioning why I wanted my space, and then breaking down and apologizing. He was thousands of miles away, but I was frightened just listening to him.

To him, it was as if I were living in a war zone, and he needed to be around me to protect me, to make sure that I ate, slept, spoke to the right people, and, above all, avoided men under all circumstances. His suspicious trait was another color of rage I had been blind to in the past. This upset me because even in my anger and doubt, I was faithful to him. After all, we were in a committed relationship. When I went out with friends, he called it Girl Power. I called it being independent. He called it "man hunting." I called it "out with the girls." To him, if any woman besides my mother or his mother was with me, it was fertile ground for me to be lured into a trap to meet someone, cheat, or be with someone he disapproved of. We began to fight. I would say, "It looks like the trust in this relationship is broken. We should part as amicable friends, respectfully." He would apologize and eventually end up calling my parents, crying, and begging them to convince me to take him back.

Everyone was growing tired of his incomprehensible behavior. After we fought, I would cry and ask him to end our engagement because I knew I would not be able to handle his behavior in heavier doses after marriage. It became impossible. Intolerably painful. The anger, the insistence, and the persistent nuisance of wanting to know everything—even why I spent too long in the bathroom—showed his lack of faith in me. His doubts were preposterous. If I wanted to speak to my friends in private, he would concoct a crazy conspiracy theory that we were up to something naughty or treacherous.

Prince Charming had turned into Crazy Cowboy, and I, who was once collected and calm, had turned into a mess. I ended it one day with a simple text message: *This is not working out. I have decided to end it for both of our sakes because I am not happy with this equation of us. Please do not contact me or my family again.*

All hell broke loose after that. The nightmare began. Someone—not Hamdan—began calling me and verbally abusing me. The stranger sent me messages saying that if I did not go back to Hamdan he would post graphically altered images of me on pornographic websites seen across the Arab world. These threats hit home, and they left me terrified. I called Hamdan to beg him to stop this madness. He feigned ignorance. His only reply to me was, "Let the man you left me for take care of you now—I'm out. Remember?"

The threats kept coming, hard and strong. The stranger would send me pictures over WhatsApp showing how he was making the alterations. He would take an image of me from a school website, crop my head, and affix it to a skinny body—or a fat one. With each passing hour, he would send me another image. The first images were cartoonish, but then they began to have fewer clothes on them and the differences in skin and body type were not as evident as before. Each fake image became more realistic. The horror of such a thing happening to you is equivalent to the tremor of an active volcano, threatening to explode at any minute. With threats pouring down on me, I sat crying, trying to think of what I could do to avert the damage. This could have ruined me. Not just my reputation, but the reputation of my entire family, could be affected.

I contacted Hamdan's family, but all of the numbers they had for him were switched off. His sisters did not know where he was, and they secretly felt bad for me. They were embarrassed to be related to such a person. He strategically removed himself from all locations where we could possibly find him and try to coax him into rectifying the situation. He would let me suffer to teach me a lesson of how weak I was without him, and, after my ruin, he would come and walk all over my bones. If he could not have me, he would merely say "I told you so" and leave me in my misery.

The blackmailer began to ask for a date in a hotel with me, instructing me to bring money. Lots of it. Anything of value—watches, jewelry, anything. As my fiancé did not want me anymore, I was fair game for this predator. I had a choice either to give in, knowing he, denying his own word, would possibly film the whole situation in order to blackmail me with more evidence, or risk the repercussions of what he would do if I continued to ignore him. After all, is there ever honor amongst thieves?

He warned me not to refuse him. He sent me images of girls who had not heeded his threats. I recognized a few faces and names of his victims, and the pictures sent shivers down my spine. These were girls from respect- able families whose faked images had been leaked to the social media, making for a slandering stock in the meat market of reputations.

I could not eat or sleep. I begged him to stop. I promised to pay him, but he wanted something to lock me down. He wanted more evidence to ruin me, and he was not afraid to say so. He sent video clips to me over the phone, and I could hear his friends in the background, laugh- ing and making jokes such as "When is the lamb coming to us wolves?" and "We'll take care of you." I had fallen into a lair of beasts, and they had no mercy whatsoever. I was so choked that I could not make myself understood when speaking to him, and my mumbling and trembling irritated him even more. At first he would laugh hysteri- cally, but then he began to put the phone down every time I called, telling me to shut up and call back when I was intelligible.

I went to the bank to cash out my accounts and give the blackmailer the money, every last dirham. I sold my jewelry to our local jeweler. He was surprised when I offered my things for sale and asked if he could keep them until I crossed whatever situation I was going through. I was touched at the kind offer from an old acquaintance. I remembered with disgust how Hamdan would say, "Men will only do you a favor if they think they can get something carnal from you." I banished Hamdan from my thoughts. Every time I banished the Devil, I banished Hamdan with him. At that time, even the Devil seemed more logical than my ex-fiancé with his twisted mind.

I hoped that selling my jewelry would at least buy me time to be able to create a larger, more lucrative pay-off. While at the jeweler's, I saw an advert for Al Ameen, a free, confidential service for blackmailed and distressed victims in Dubai. It was a new secret service established for people who could not tell their families about their situation for fear of hurting them. The advert said Al Ameen helped women threatened by unscrupulous villains trying to extort them by exploiting their fears of being publicly declared a loose woman and having their social standing destroyed. It was an answer to my prayers. I jumped at the chance to escape my doom. That simple advert lit a candle of hope in my heart.

Even so, I was nervous about calling. It hurts to admit that you have gotten yourself into such a compromising position. As soon as I spoke with an investigator, I broke down and begged him to help me. I spilled the story and desperately asked for help. The private detective insisted on meeting me face to face.

"Is that really necessary?" I asked. "Can't I just forward the texts?"

"I'm sorry," said the private detective. "We have to interview you to substantiate your claims. You would be surprised how many people fake harassment just to get sympathy or get men into trouble."

I found it hard to believe that anyone would willingly pretend to be going through the nightmare I so desperately wanted to end.

"Never underestimate the human need for attention," said the detective. "There wouldn't be an entertainment industry without it—ha, ha, ha."

I met with the detective the next day. He wanted to see the threats, so I showed him the texts. He asked to hear the video message with the howling wolves, and I played it. But when he wanted to see the graphically altered images, I demurred. My blackmailer had said that he was going to search through the millions of porn videos and eventually find someone that looked like me and then post it on YouTube, claiming it was me. Even if he did not have to alter the face, the coupling of my name to a girl with similar features was enough to taint me. A girl's reputation is all she has, which is why it is guarded jealously and she is covered so modestly—to protect her reputation and the reputation of her family.

"Do you have a female investigator on your staff?" I asked.

"Yes," he said. "Why?"

"I would rather show the photos to her."

"I understand," said the detective.

Even at that, I deleted the photos that even slightly resembled me. I did not care if it weakened my case. It was too embarrassing to have anyone see them, even someone who wanted to help me. I shuddered when I thought about how I would feel if the images were ever posted online. What if they wanted to keep copies of these images for future use or, alternatively, if someone from the detective's family or one of her acquaintances came to know about it?

Convinced by my demeanor, the consistency of my answers, and the overwhelming amount of evidence I presented, the detectives agreed to help me. They advised me to tell the blackmailer that I would go ahead with his plan, just as he demanded.

My father was not informed of the details of what was happening; he only knew that I had received threats and that Hamdan was nowhere to be found. However, my mother and elder sister knew and feared for my safety and sanity. I informed my mother of what Al Ameen had said and she was in the car waiting outside the Mirage Hotel in Dubai where I had agreed to meet the blackmailer. I brought a suitcase packed with cash, as promised. What he did not know was that the police were everywhere dressed as civilians, laughing, chatting, and doing what people in a hotel normally do. They were going to tail us and step in as he received the money, capturing him and, hopefully, his accomplices.

Fearing a trap, the blackmailer told me to follow him to another location. He was smart, but I had done my homework. I had been cornered and tortured, and I was genuinely frightened. My fingers would not stop twitching. I informed the police of what was happening through the bug they placed on my earring. When I asked why they put it there, they casually said it was in case I had to leave my car or my bag, or if my clothes were removed. This practical consideration terrified me.

I drove behind the man who had taunted and terrorized me, following his black Range Rover in my blue-tinted Bentley. The police followed at a distance to avoid detection. I smiled inside to think that the hunter was walking into a trap of his own making. The end could not come soon enough. I was finally going to be released from this prison of madness. I wanted nothing to do with this pack of animals.

He pulled his Range Rover into the Grosvenor House hotel. My cheeks were wet with tears. I was crying out of hope that the nightmare would soon end and out of fear that it might not. I kept my hands on the steering wheel the whole way, afraid that wiping my face would cause the car to swerve in a way that would raise his suspicions. From the way he kept glancing in his rearview mirror and making turn after unnecessary turn, I sensed he was jittery. I struggled to control myself. As I stepped out of the car with my suitcase filled with cash, I covered my face. I did not want him to see that I had been crying, even if it was from relief.

I walked into the hotel and saw him. He was a tall, handsome man with a cheeky goatee. He was wearing dark glasses even though it was 8 pm. In his white thobe he looked to me like Lucifer. I had so much fear and hatred for this cruel man that I did not know how to act. My legs froze, and I just stood there, staring at him. Finally he crossed the lobby to collect me, grabbing my hand and dragging me with him. In the elevator he thanked me for covering my face, so no one would recognize me with him. Then he laughed and said, "If you haven't brought enough money, I can always uncover your face and make my millions."

"Why . . . why are you doing this? I never did anything to you." I could not imagine how much ugliness resided in him. "Is Hamdan here? Does he know what's going on? Please take your money and disappear. Please."

The lift arrived at his floor too soon. My calm was replaced with panic.

Shaking from fear, I was dragged along behind him. I shot furtive glances up and down the halls, hoping to spot a police officer. Something was wrong. Where were the police? When we got to the room, I refused to go in. Something was amiss. The past few nights of little sleep were taking a toll on my strength and reason. There were no police. What if this madman raped me and the police showed up afterwards? What if he captured it on video? I would rather die.

"Just take the money and give me my pictures," I begged him.

He just smiled as he swiped the door key and then yanked me into the room. He jerked the suitcase out of my hand and pushed me onto the bed. I knew what was coming next. *Not without a fight, where I rip you to pieces,* I thought. He put his hands up to lift his thobe from above, and I rolled off the bed, falling clumsily to the floor. My knees were jelly. There was nowhere to go.

That is when I saw someone grab the blackmailer from behind and throw him onto the floor. When I heard the click of the handcuffs, I knew my nightmare was over.

"Where did you come from?" I asked the police officer. He explained that when I had stopped in the lobby, my legs refusing to move, he had quietly approached the desk clerk. The clerk identified the man in the lobby who approached me and gave the officer a key to his room. The officer was already in the room when my blackmailer dragged me inside. The scene of the swarming police with me on the floor crying from relief was a fitting end to all of my past tears. The horror was real; I could feel, see, and smell it. I tasted blood in my mouth because I had bitten my own lip in terror.

I thanked the officer and simply sat on the floor, thanking the Lord for His mercy. I had had enough electric shocks. I have no doubt my tormentor planned to shoot a video of him raping me to continually use against me. I kept thinking of his enormous strength when he had pulled me into the room. I never felt so helpless in my life. I would have fought him, but it would have been useless.

The blackmailer was sentenced to five years in prison. My ex-fiancé was tried as an accomplice, since he had told his friend to do his worst to me. He was acquitted, but was forced to do fifty hours of social work and undergo therapeutic and psychiatric help, and he remains unmarried. He has apologized to me several times, but I keep my distance from him. I have blocked him on all of my social media networks and phones. The blackmailer remains in prison.

I went back to university and got a master's degree in psychology, as I felt the need to better understand human behavior. I am grateful to the Al Ameen service that saved my life, my honor, my future, and my sanity.

The Apple of My Eye

I AM A PERFECTIONIST. I strive to be the best there is and I work really, really hard. Working hard teaches one how to appreciate practice, and the reward is success. I learned all I know from my mother, who was one of the few women of her generation to finish her college education and work full time. She was employed first in a school and then in the Ministry of Education whilst being a mother, and did so immaculately. The workaholic in her did not allow her to slack off in her home duties. She and my father were diligent about having a wholesome family and would spend time with us daily on developing our skills, studies, and personalities.

We were an average-sized family of two boys and one girl. My mother loved her children very much and invested all her spare time in them, especially her daughter. She wanted me, her beloved daughter, to be especially success-ful, beautiful and accomplished, and that I was. I was her dream created and realized. I aspired to exceed my mother's expectations and always make her proud. She was the envy of every mother, and I, the daughter, wanted nothing but to make her proud.

I eventually was engaged to a distant cousin who was my first crush as a child. My friends and I referred to him as Mr Heartthrob. Naturally, I was thrilled that he expressed an interest in tying the knot with me as soon as he graduated from his university in the United States. I was studying at Qatar University and very much looking forward to being Mrs Heartthrob.

I had a calendar of to-dos, as most brides do. I began working on my skin, hair, body, and nails; my wedding planning included flowers, favors, the guest list (friends, relatives, the ones I wanted, and the ones I did not want but had to invite anyway), the after party, the honeymoon, the bridesmaids, their dresses, crowns, the entertainment at the wedding and the parties—the list went on and on. I enjoyed every moment of organizing the wedding, so much so that I even thought of starting up my own wedding planning business after it was over. I had a knack for it, being detail-oriented and willing to research every minute necessity and luxury in the process of planning a project.

I was always Skyping with my fiancé, Jassim, keeping him entertained with my daily adventures. Everything was proceeding according to plan. I was so happy I felt like an over-inflated balloon that would burst at any moment. My family and friends would always tell me I should give thanks to God for being this happy and for everything working out so smoothly.

My wedding was at a beautiful time of year, when spring is ending but summer has not yet begun. The weather was pleasant. The guests coming from neighboring countries would not be too troubled because I specifically booked it post-school and pre-summer travels, when there is an exodus of Gulf Arabs leaving to Europe, Asia, and Africa.

My mother had a dress made by Reem Acra New York and wore Badgley Mischka shoes. Her gown looked like something that Audrey Hepburn would wear, which suited her, as she was naturally slim and tall. Her winged eyeliner made her look like Marilyn Monroe, with her mole in the same spot and her hair the lightest it had ever been.

My gown was Elie Saab, majestic and grand. When I tried it on for the first time, I had not slept in days and was nervous that the gown would look too sexy for a saintly bride. Mother cried when she saw how beautiful I looked in it. We hugged, and I cried and told her how much I loved her and how everything I had become was because she loved me that much.

My friends and cousins were all dressed just as stylishly, because everyone knew that if you were coming to my wedding you were expected to be dressed to the nines. And dressed to the nines they were. I commended and complimented everyone, and we took pictures so we could always look back at this beautiful day.

We had Hussain Al Jassimi, a popular Khaleeji singer, sing our favorite songs. My mother went on and on about me saying my prayers, because I looked like an angel. The makeup artist was applying my makeup and telling wild stories about what the evil eye had done to people she knew personally. There were stories of people breaking their heels, falling, getting a burn, and other unfortuitous events. There was a tale of a man who could down a helicopter with his evil eye. Another about how a woman got pregnant seven times, and each time gave birth to a stillborn perfect baby. Mother was fearful for me and was telling everyone to bless me and remember that all the beauty I had was from God.

I had said my prayers enough times that I did not have stage fright. I felt safe. I walked down the aisle, sat on the sofa, and looked upon my guests in the full ballroom. But then, all of a sudden, with no warning, the brightly lit ballroom went black. I could hear music and voices, but I could not see anyone or anything. No color, no shadow, no light. Pitch black. I blinked and blinked, but the darkness remained.

The noise of the celebration loud in my ears, I stretched out my hands until I felt a hand that I recognized from its softness as my mother's. I almost fell from the chaise lounge, where I had been waiting for my husband to take pictures with me and carry me away to Paris.

I felt clumsy and handicapped at how much I needed my sight, even for balance. I wasn't scared; I was terrified. I needed an explanation. I felt an arm around my waist and I recognized my maid's voice, asking me how I could trip while sitting down. I began crying and told her I could not see her. Why had they switched off the lights?

She asked me again and again if I could see, but I could not. My adrenaline kicked in, and I could not understand her explanations. I wanted to run, to gasp for air; perhaps outside the streetlights were on, and that would restore my sanity and calm my fright.

No one goes blind all of a sudden. Unheard of. Simply plain mad. I did not even wear glasses. I had gone to a doctor only once for my eyes, when I had conjunctivitis at twelve years old. I never wore contacts for vision, although I had once tried colored contacts for a picture years before. I suffered no ailments worth mentioning. I needed my mother, I needed my husband, I needed everyone to hold me, to tell me it was a bad joke and that it was fixable. I wanted it to be something science could explain and correct. Panic, shock, bacteria, a virus—something that surgery, medicine, or even psychological therapy could reverse.

My mother began reading verses of the Qur'an and, after ten minutes, when nothing happened, she requested that the gates be closed and that everyone in the ballroom come and bless me because it seemed that an evil eye had struck me. The music stopped, replaced by loud whispers about this cruel strike of fate. Someone had looked at me with so much envy that it was like a spell cast on me that blinded me. Usually if such a thing happened, it was milder: an eye infection or failing eyesight that might require glasses. But this was an extreme case. Things like these did not happen to normal people like me, and especially not on my wedding day and in public. The tragic comedy of my situation left me in tears. I wanted and needed to understand what was going on.

Logic left the hall, and everyone began paying advice and panicking. I could hear murmurs, weeping, and whispers. People began calling God's name and asking for mercy. All of this made me nervous and scared. I began to realize I might never again see my family's faces, my husband's face as he spoke comforting words to me, my future children; all of these thoughts drowned me. They felt like waves crashing over me again and again, reminding me that I would never see the birthday cakes I would attempt to make (or buy and act like I made because I knew the technique). I would not be able to look at people's faces to see if they believed me or not, and then their expressions after I burst out laughing because I was kidding.

I shut my eyes, knit my brows, and opened my eyes again as wide as I could, and still I could not see. I was drowning, but I was on the wedding sofa, beseeching my mother and husband to help me. Tears ran down my cheeks, neck, and chest, and I did not care anymore about the pretty pictures or what people saw and thought. They were strong, smart, dependable people, and they would know what to do. Everything can be fixed if we try.

My husband was in the ballroom by now and tried to soothe my worries, saying that if it came on suddenly, it might disappear suddenly. I could not see—not now and maybe never again. So why should I care? I wept until I felt faint and my husband carried me away. He tried to reassure me, and I wanted to believe him. I made him promise that he would do his utmost to help me regain my sight and to understand why this had happened.

We changed our honeymoon trip from France to Germany to visit the doctors there, as they are highly respected. I went to sleep in tears on my wedding night, thinking about how my perfect day had been ruined. Jassim tried everything to console me. He told me how much he loved me and how we were married and he was happy and all that mattered was that we were together, man and wife, and all would be resolved in due time. For the first few nights, we lay together like virgin lovers, and he would whisper sweet nothings and promises that his heart would not change toward me. These words meant so much to the blind perfectionist who had lost her crown on her coronation day. He was gentle and kind, and I was grateful for the gift of having a rock to lean on when fate had been so cruel to me.

It pained me that I could not see him. He told me to use my fingers to see him. I was a child, learning to see the world in a different way. It was slow, but intense. The suggestive nature of how the cheek protrudes, the lips curve, the short facial hair prickles, the limbs quiver, and the breath quickens into short gasps was as alluring as it was stimulating. I was eager to soon see and enjoy the full view of my experience with my better half.

He believed my condition was treatable, and I believed him, because I would have killed myself then and there had I known I was going to be diagnosed with dead optic cells once I arrived in Germany. The tests were too many, and the results were too slow. I heard too much foreign scientific language and too little hope in it. The daily tests were becoming mundane and maddening with their dead-end findings. I was fully analyzed. They tested my head, hair, history, DNA, teeth, kidneys, sugar levels, blood pressure, heart, brain functions, and bodily functions. They found other minor things wrong with me, but nothing to do with my eyes.

They treated my stressed shoulders, which I think were due to the wedding preparations. I had low iron, and that was treated with a diet of more liver, spinach, and beetroot. I began gentle exercise with a coach and started seeing a psychiatrist. They tried to find out if my loss of vision was a deep-rooted, psychological problem. They even thought I was imagining it, willing it, or a really talented actress. A foolish attempt to shock me by telling me that my family had died in a car accident left me crying and shivering. It did not work, and I did not appreciate it. I was reduced to a mere piece of a human being—someone who felt defeated, damaged and handicapped.

Our perfect Eiffel Tower park strolls and Cannes beach trips were exchanged for medical wards, MRIs, doctors, eye specialists, and psychoanalysts. I came home after three or four months, still blind and feeling sorry that I was never going to read a book, paint a picture, take a photograph, or even sit back and select the picture that I would want hanging in our bedroom of us standing together as man and wife.

I suffered from such deep depression that I was put on antidepressants. I eventually grew used to sitting with old women, having tea and reminiscing about the old days. Old people often discuss the beautiful old days and what they saw. That was a conversation I could participate in wholeheartedly. I learned to "see" people from the way they spoke, the words they chose, and the rush or patience they had in divulging their emotions. How they began and ended their tales told me how they felt about their stories and illustrated all that I could not see with my eyes.

My group of friends grew smaller as I could no longer participate in their lively social gatherings. I could hear their pity and their exaggerated descriptions of what was going on. At first, I tried to stay engaged, but I no longer could enjoy movies, coffee shops, or restaurants. I could not participate in discussions about their Photoshopped pictures, before and after; the poetry and jokes they would send via WhatsApp; the shopping for dresses, jewelry, and accessories; and all of the details of the things I used to thrive on. I was blind, and that was that. I could not see what they were describing, and the extra effort required for me to understand seemed, after a time, as burdensome for me to hear as it was on them to explain.

I felt myself withering away. Everyone slowly distanced themselves from me except for my two closest friends and my sister. All I had was them and my mother, who stood by me more than she needed to and kept me strong. She was heartbroken and would often cry, but she understood me best. She always held my hand gently and would tell me where to set foot, should there be an unstable way or staircase. She would explain things succinctly enough for me to understand the silence in a gathering or a loud noise in the crowd: "Laila is joking"; "Spectacular fireworks"; "Lovely children, come say hello to me and Aunty." She was my only solace. She made me feel normal. She would encourage me by reading stories about successful blind people to me. She even taught me how to read in Braille.

She would invite my friends over once a month, which was enough excitement for me and not too much trouble for them. They would call more often than visit, as my hearing was fine and they knew that talking on the phone was something I could really enjoy. I also began to enjoy the Turkish television series as I learned to recognize the voices. My ears became my new eyes, and I was grateful for the savior. I was afraid of leaving my home because I had tripped and hurt myself so many times. I tried hard to climb out from the hole that I was in, but it was too deep, even for someone as hardheaded as I am. I began to listen to audiobooks, which entertained me and became a hobby that I enjoyed immensely. It helped both to compensate for lost reading time and to help me heal.

Despite these gains, it still hurt when cruel and heartless people pitied my husband for being married to a blind woman. As my hearing developed, I regularly heard whispers of "poor bloke," "she can't see anything," and "I wonder if her kids will be born blind." I would bristle every time. You never get used to cruelty, especially when it makes you feel like you are an injustice to the people you love.

My husband felt cheated and decided that he had come up short someplace. Several times I asked for a divorce, but he refused. He spoke from an emotional and religious standpoint, stating that he loved me and swearing to stand by me. Divorcing me would indicate dissatisfaction with God's gift to him, be it favorable or unfavorable in its outcome. He was God fearing, and I had hope that just as God had given me sight, and had taken it, that He would give it back one day soon.

I could not dress as fashionably and daring as I liked. I could not see my face so I resigned myself to wearing minimal makeup. Even then, there was no way to tell if I was wearing a blue blusher or a coral eye shadow by mistake. I could still wear my matte Chanel lipstick; do my basic eye makeup of an eye pencil lining my eyes, the simple tapping of the YSL mascara wand against my lashes, and the patting of my Guerlain face powder on my combination, T-zone skin. I refused to look pale and plain. I would always ask several people to give me their opinions of my makeup. Simple and clean, the chances of messing it up were almost zero.

Eventually, I began to tire of the simple look, but the holy ritual of applying red lipstick after maroon lip liner, slightly tipping over your natural Cupid's bow and lower lip to give the illusion of bee-stung lips, was no longer natural to me. The art of pampering myself, applying face-masks and tweezing my eyebrows, were complex tasks that required a makeup artist to help me with, so I began requesting home service. I may have been blind, but my military-like discipline prevented me from allowing myself to have a disheveled appearance.

I still insisted on wearing jewelry and perfume, however basic or inexpensive, but pearls were my favorite. I was a lady, and I always liked to look prim and proper. In my former presentation, I derived the confidence of a peacock from my assurance that I was the fittest, most finely dressed, and best educated woman in my batch—the unbeatable perfection that I always had been.

My mother would cry sometimes; I could hear her voice break when she would see beautiful things, like every time my babies were born, or, as the years passed, when they would draw hearts and happy faces with "I Love You Mummy." My ears began to detect all of the emotional notes in a person's voice. I could tell when they were lying, smiling, hesitant, scared, doubtful, hateful, or envious. My mother said that what had happened to me was an evil eye that was envious of how perfect I was. I was not perfect anymore, so I presumed I would carry on like this until my dying day. She explained that living in gratitude causes good things to happen and it acts as a tourniquet to staunch the calamities that befall us.

Of all the sounds I heard, the most joyous came on the day I heard my first-born cry. I snuggled him and I instantly loved him. After he was bathed and cleaned, they brought him to me to feed, and I had a reason to live again. I was so full of emotion and hope; I wanted to "see" him live to be the best there was in life. I felt like the rising sun. After they told me his sight was fine, I did not care that I was blind. The terror of childbirth was multiplied in my situation, because I could not help myself or my baby. He could be bleeding and hurting, and I would not know. I had all my next children by Caesarian section because during normal childbirth the adrenaline rose so much in my blood it distressed the baby.

This new object of my affection was so precious and filled me with so much happiness, a feeling that I had lost and missed very much. It rekindled my life with my husband, as he was very supportive of me throughout my ordeal. I fell in love with him all over again because he was my hero. You never really know a man until you become handicapped and completely dependent upon him; that is the true test of a man to see whether or not he is someone you would want to grow old with.

However, this only added to the pressure I felt to be good enough. If only my sight were to come back, I could perform my day-to-day activities more normally. I recognized my son's smell and his calls, and I tried to do as many things on my own with him as I could, because he was my new obsession. My husband would tell me it was not fair that the child looked exactly like me, and I would smile at how supportive he was.

Jassim, always solid, at times would lose patience with my moping attitude. I would dive into an abyss of depression whenever I got hormonal in my pregnancy. I had nightmares that were too real, dreaming that the baby would be born with sealed sockets where its eyes should be.

I missed the wasted time talking nonsense to myself in the mirror, imagining scenarios with the people I loved talking to and admiring me and the people I hated eyeing me, and what I would say preposterously in response. Men do not have these minutes of escape we women do. This is our therapy, our reward for looking good: to first feast our own eyes on the accomplishment we have done to ourselves.

I resented how people always asked me if I had found a solution to my sight loss. I woke up every day with that loss, how could I ever lose *sight* of it? I fought and I tried, if only to be the shadow of the person that I once was. I wanted to be happy for my Jassim and my four angels. I could hear my mother's voice crack when she talked about my amazing accomplishments and then slowly trail away and choke as she quietly wiped her tears. It was interesting how I could foretell situations from how they started, how people concocted conversations to reach a point where it was only logical to ask me invasive personal questions. And I, in turn, always rose to the occasion, answering them quickly and abruptly, or simply leaving the sly crowd. These times invested with the social groups benefited my family. I became more forgiving, measured, and grateful for the enjoyment of normalcy I once had.

When God takes something from you, He usually gives you something else in return. We never found out what happened to my eyes, but I learned to be grateful for the many beautiful things that I had in life. I bore Jassim four children. We did not travel the first two or three years, but after I had my children back-to-back and they were older, we began to travel to the English countryside. The children loved it, and I did not have to worry about the traffic for my own safety or the children running off into a busy street. My husband and I relaxed and enjoyed our time together.

We would sometimes attempt to see a doctor or two. I visited Mecca every year and washed my face with Zamzam holy water, hoping it would return my sight to me. I attempted Chinese medicine. Needles were inserted into my skull, neck, and back, but to no avail. I accepted my blindness, but I never stopped trying to recover my sight. How could I? I wanted to see the faces of my children. I wanted to see how badly they had cut themselves when they would come to me crying from a fall. I wanted to see if they were dressed properly and eating what they had on their plates. I wanted to read to them and see their faces light up, or watch them fall asleep as I told them stories from memory.

My fingers would run along their profiles and faces; this was my face shot of them. My hands measured when it was time to cut their hair and if their clothes were thick enough for the weather outside. It was humiliating, but I was strong for them. Not for me, not for my husband, not for my family, but for my children. It was all for them. I loved them so much. They made me feel so strong and so weak at the same time, but I fought for them.

One day, I woke up in a room filled with bright light and color. My eyesight was back, just as suddenly as it had disappeared. Of course, I did not recognize my surroundings. I began looking at everything in the house, running (something I had not done in years) and calling after everyone in the house.

I called my mother with the joyous news, but she did not answer. I called my mother every day, or she would call me, to check on each other. I knew from my voice clock that it was noon, and, knowing she was an early riser, I began to worry. But I was so excited that I put aside my fears.

Everything looked different. There was so much color and light. I swam through it like a fish in water. I could not close my eyes. I called my brother, laughing hysterically, and told him I could see. I could see everything: the chair, the phone, and the pictures of these beautiful children who must be mine! I was too busy describing the things around me to hear his response. I was a volcano of energy that needed attention, and I wanted the whole world to know about this blessing. My brother said he was happy for me, but I detected something serious in his tone of voice. I had spoken so fast that he could not interrupt to explain why Mother had not been answering.

"Ameera," he said at last, "Mother is dead."

I stopped jumping and sat down.

My sister had just pulled into the driveway. She walked in on me and hugged me. "He giveth and He taketh away," she whispered.

Speechless. Numb. Mixed emotions. Confused. Where was I? What was going on on this Earth? Mother would be so disappointed to have left this world thinking she left behind a blind daughter. She deserved to know that I was okay. I was angry that she had passed without forewarning. How ridiculously selfish of me, but this is life, a play that makes us both laugh and cry.

Jassim was on a business trip to Washington DC. I did not know how to send a text message, as it had been a good few years and I needed to be updated and shown how to write again. Braille never got to mobiles, so I asked my sister to text him for me.

My grandmother and sister insisted that I visit the doctors, religious folks, and psychiatrists immediately. The doctors were more confused than I was. The very same doctors I recognized from their shuffling footsteps, perfume, breath, and tone of voice now seemed so magnified with sight. I could hear the hesitation in their voices, and all they would say was "Thank Goodness" and smile nervously.

I next went to the religious folks, and they began to recite holy verses and bless me. Then they asked about my circumstances and what had changed. I told them of my mother's death, and a sad silence descended. They explained that sometimes too much love and pride in your possessions could actually hurt that very thing you hold so dear. I needed to hear it from three or four different pious, saintly,

God-fearing people to fully understand it. My mother had loved me very much, so much so that I could feel and sense every meaning of the word. She did not know that her doting pride in me, multiplied with admiration, was to be my undoing. I was her Achilles heel of self-worth, self-image, and self-regard, but I was not she; I was someone else. The master's creation had surpassed the master, and she unknowingly envied it.

I sat with the psychiatrist for an hour-long session of lamenting my loss of sight for years, grieving my mother, and complaining how my whole world had come undone. I left weeping, and a nurse was sent home to take care of me and monitor my stability. I was given an injection to calm me down at the insistence of my sister, who terrified me with the thought that if I did not cooperate, my brain would pop. I conceded, but I was trembling. I was feeling guilty and sad at how happy I was, and I bemoaned the loss of my mother. She had been my walking stick, my eyes, my patient senses throughout these years. I missed her. She left a canyon of grief so deep and gaping that not even my regained sight could bridge it.

The carnival that was going on in my life was enough to give a grown elephant a heart attack, so I sat down and wept. The day I got my sight back, I cried more than I had cried on any day in my life. There was so much to capture, and I treasured everything. I almost did not recognize myself in the mirror. The recollection of who I had been and the need to accept who this new woman was overwhelmed me. I had to use drops to lubricate my eyes because I could not stop staring. I was excited by the realization that I was capable of seeing my own hands, the next step I would take in confidence and safety. I was overwhelmed with beautiful feelings and gratitude, and I lost myself in prayer.

Jassim flew in to the Doha airport, and I went to collect him with my sister. He looked almost the same as he had on our wedding day, with just a few odd white hairs above his ears. He was a little heavier, and I was shy to even hug him until I recognized his smell, his voice, and the energy he gave me when we were together. I was a bundle of mixed feelings: Accepting the new, older face of the man I had been intimate with for years was a huge emotional challenge.

The children. Oh, the children were perfect, just as I had imagined them to be, although I did not recognize them until my fingers scanning them told me who they were. I familiarized myself with how they looked, but I was in the habit of feeling their faces and they connected to that. Even to this day, years later, they take my hands gently and allow my fingers to trail their features. It was a habit they had grown to love. When they would hug me, they would notice me breathing deeper to take in their smell. I would hear them first, the pitter patter of small feet, the rushed steps of my son, the dragging swagger of my other son, the gentle and quiet steps of my daughter, and the flippity flap of the maids' fast steps. I recognized the way their arms brushed against their bodies and the way that they would sit down: some quietly, some collapsing into the chair, and some in their own fidgety way. I felt each one's energy, and they used to make jokes at how Mummy could *see* from their energy. The way they breathed and the way they spoke was my polygraph of their emotional and physical state.

The overwhelming feelings left me restless and fearful that I would lose my sight again. The doctors did not have an answer the second time around either. This was worse. I needed to have an answer, and I went to several specialists. I wanted science to justify my unjust imprisonment in darkness, and I wanted reassurance that it would not return.

At my mother's funeral, I stood silent. I did not announce that my sight had returned because I wanted the funeral to be my mother's final goodbye, not a celebration of the return of my sight.

I was ignored because everyone thought I still was blind. I tried to control my alert eyes, which were darting back and forth, measuring, calculating, drinking up the faces and how they had aged; the colors and artistry of the objects that surrounded us; the furniture design; and even the presentation of the food. I could see, and I wanted to see every single detail of everything.

Afterwards, my grandmother told me that sometimes when a mother loves her child too much and gloats about it, she actually gives it the evil eye. My mother loved me very much and was very critical of anything lacking in me. I was the apple of her eye, and it was out of her love that an arrow had hit me, blinding me.

The way the evil eye is treated depends on the strength of that negative energy. No wonder my many trips to doctors and religious folk never yielded any result. The only cure for my blindness was the death of the person who had given me the look of envious admiration: my poor, unknowing mother.

The Grass on the Other Side

A T FORTY-TWO YEARS OLD, Saad was an average-looking government employee in Riyadh. His life was a drab routine of work, sleep, watching television with his wife and five children, and going to occasional gatherings with his friends in the evenings. He and his wife of seventeen years, Huda, had settled into a comfortable life and understood each other well—perhaps too well, to the point where theirs had become a mundane, sparkleless marriage. For many years, Huda had been proud of her husband's success in finding a stable position with the government; it meant that the threats of unemployment and spinsterhood had been handled. However, she was becoming increasingly dissatisfied that his career was going nowhere. The family wanted more of life's luxuries, and those came at a price.

Once a slender beauty, Huda had let herself go. As her looks faded, so did her interest in making herself look good. With the children's never-ending wants and the lack of time to do all the things they had to do, she had to prioritize. She stopped wearing makeup, fixing her hair, dressing up, and wearing alluring fragrances.

Saad would often think about the early days of marriage and how exciting and beautiful his wife had been. The children had become too much work and too much trouble—for her and for him. Life at home demanded a constant attention that was unappreciated and thankless. The stress was unwelcome, but withstood, because it was a responsibility that had to be handled, and Saad was a responsible man. He knew the rules and he abided by them religiously.

During coffee breaks at work, Saad and his coworkers sat in the coffee shop and discussed stocks, cars, Iran and its nuclear ambitions, travel, shopping in the United States, food, and women. Often the talk would turn to taking a second wife, especially the practice of doing it the *mesyar* way. *Mesyar* means "to visit" in Arabic. This kind of marriage was promoted in the old days as a way of helping women who needed support—usually widows who needed a man for financial assistance, or as a presence for her children, or to act as a face for her business, or to meet her needs away from sin.

Nowadays, *mesyar* marriages were nothing more than legal flings with no strings attached, like a brief stay at a hotel. Such marriages did not involve children and payments were at the discretion of the husband. There was no public scandal and no unhappy first wife, because she would be oblivious to what was happening. Furthermore, there would be no community judging the selected fruit of the man's passion or rejecting his "lower status" wife. Nothing but a happy man getting the best of both worlds.

Dr Jekyll during the day and Mr Hyde at night. These men usually kept the other woman a secret, preferring not to publicize the *mesyar* marriage.

"What wife number one does not know will not hurt her," joked one of Saad's friends.

"That's right," said another friend. "The second is for pleasure only. With no children involved, no one is left feeling hurt or cheated. It's a win-win situation. Even your first wife will be secretly delighted that you have let go of your tightness and stress. You both will be more satisfied."

"But it must remain a secret," added a third.

Everyone at some point thinks of the grass on the other side of the fence, whether it is just a one-night stand, a short affair, or a secret marriage. Saad and his friends all feared God, but they also feared rocking their stable domestic ship. To be married would guarantee that the woman was only yours, because you married her. To have an affair could be a curse, because the mistress could be promiscuous, and that made the men nervous. They did not have time to waste investing in and supporting someone who was not their own. She would be simply for his pleasure, just as he would be for hers—nothing more. Sordid, maybe, but the woman needed it as much as the man did, and they would have an understanding.

Listening to chitchat like this on a daily basis can shake even the sturdiest of ships.

"But how to get away from your family?" Saad wondered aloud one day.

"You can always find a reason," said one of the older men, sagely.

Saad often wondered if this man had a *mesyar* marriage.

"Take up falconry or hunting—something that takes you to the desert on weekends. Women love breaks from their husbands. Just leave her extra money, and she will keep herself busy. Besides, you're the man in the relationship."

Another friend chimed in: "Then there are holidays. You let the wife and children go ahead by a few days. You tell them something came up at the office, but you do not want to spoil their vacation."

A Filipino waiter brought a coffee to the table, murmuring something about extra sugar for someone and other niceties. Quick thank-yous were exchanged, and the men went back to discussing the fine details of their master plans for a second heaven on earth.

"A beautiful woman will bring out your creativity," said one of Saad's friends, eyeing a girl in a magazine. "I want one that looks like this Lebanese singer, only I want her fatter. Divorced women with kids have better bodies and fewer demands; they would do it because they need someone to pay the bills. They do not mind it being secret, either. Besides, women cannot live without men. God will favor you saving a poor, helpless widow or a starving divorcee from the painful life of being single. I once married a widow who did not have kids, which was perfect for a few years. She had fifteen cats, and her cats hated me because I was king."

Everyone laughed.

114

"Then she wanted to ruin it by having kids, but I refused. I told her, 'Your cats are your kids. Why add more siblings?!'"

This comment brought even more laughter.

"She left to Australia to study and at first she used to call, but now I guess she has moved on. At least she took her mangy cats with her!" He rolled his eyes, raised his eyebrows high, and laughed to make it look like a trivial affair.

"What are you worried about?" another friend teased Saad. "Do you really think Huda is going to suspect you of having another woman? As long as your household is taken care of money-wise and you come home at night, that is enough."

Everyone laughed, even Saad. He secretly wondered if he was the only one without a *mesyar* wife. Had he been slow to hop on the bandwagon of happy husbands and secret wives?

"You do not want one of these girls," said the sage, pointing at the girls in the magazine with too much makeup, colored hair piled too high, and lips like goldfish. "You go to sleep with Aisha and wake up next to Fatima, and you wonder what happened to her face while you were asleep."

The group erupted in laughter, drawing the attention of the other patrons.

"Why have a fling when you can have something legal, something dependable, something entirely yours? And it is legal. *Halal*. God will not punish you. Your wife does not have a right to get upset, because it was done under the eye and allowance of God. You will have no shortcomings."

"But where would you find a good one?" Saad asked the older man.

His friend gave him a smile and mouthed the word "matchmaker."

The younger, humorous one began singing, "Matchmaker, matchmaker, please find me a wife. I want her tall, with rosy cheeks and money bags, and her hands will cook me my tummy's delight."

These conversations were enjoyable, and excitement was building up inside Saad. His friends promised to chip in with gifts for the *mesyar* wife and the dowry. They even offered to loan him their cars, holiday homes, and expensive items such as watches, cufflinks, and pens to impress the woman.

That afternoon, Saad received an email from his older office mate with the subject line, *MM*. It listed four women and gave their phone numbers. At the bottom of the list, his friend had typed, *Good luck, Groom*.

Saad entered the names and numbers into his phone. It was his right. One woman is simply not enough. A man has needs. He needs new blood every once in a while. It is his reward for working so hard.

When he got to his car after work, he called the first name on the list. An older woman answered.

"*Salam*, my sister, are you a matchmaker?" Saad asked, quieter than he normally spoke, the phone trembling in his hand. It was really happening. He was going to do it.

"Yes, brother, how can I help you?" said the woman. She waited for his response.

"I am looking for a *mesyar* marriage," said Saad, trying to sound suave and confident. He forgot the sentences he had prepared, but managed to say how the marriage had to be absolutely secret, the bride had to be beautiful with a good figure, and preferably had to be from a faraway area and a family that did not mix with his family's circles.

"I see," said the matchmaker. She did not sound friendly after he spoke the word *mesyar*. Saad realized that she probably was stereotyping him. He wanted to tell her that he was not ugly, fat, or poor. He could afford a new bride, but he had good reasons for wanting a secret arrangement.

"How old are you?"

"Forty-two."

"How long have you been married?"

"Seventeen years."

"Do you want this to be arranged discreetly?"

"Yes. Absolutely," said Saad. He almost laughed with relief.

"How much do you have for a dowry?"

That was unexpected. "Um. What is the average?"

"Average? Do you want someone who is average?"

"Well, no," Saad stuttered. He wanted someone who looked like a beauty queen, only heavier and cheap, but he dared not say it aloud.

"I probably can find a good match for you for about 30,000. If you were young and handsome, I could find you an older wife who could take care of you. But you are too old and poor."

It was more than Saad was expecting, but he had more than enough money in a government retirement account to cover it.

"I'm a good-looking man. I'm tall, I play basketball, and I'm fair. People take me for a royal all the time because of my looks," said Saad, defending himself.

"Perhaps so, but she will not be young for what you are willing to pay," said the matchmaker. "If you want someone much younger than yourself, you're talking 50 to 60,000 minimum."

"No, no, not young," said Saad. "But is there anyone thirty-five to forty, at least?"

The matchmaker laughed. "Don't worry; I won't fix you up with anyone my age." She sounded like she was in her late fifties and spoke with years of experience.

"I need to see her first," Saad said.

"Of course," said the matchmaker. She seemed to understand who he was and what he wanted. In fact, he was embarrassed at how well she understood him.

"I take fifty percent of the dowry," said the matchmaker. "It is my gift."

Saad agreed to meet the matchmaker to discuss the details further. She instructed him to bring a sack of rice, a jar of honey, and random groceries when he came to her home. He sat there wondering how many men had fetched her groceries and if this would be a common practice until she found him a decent, tailor-fitted wife.

While he was at the supermarket he shopped for desert trip groceries: wood for the fire, thick desert carpets, coal for cooking, ground coffee and large water bottles. He bought a DVD for his son, a makeup tutorial for his wife, Miss Dior perfume for his elder daughter, and salt-and-vinegar chips for his youngest daughter. The little one loved chips, and he loved giving her little gifts. Children were so easy to please, and cheaper too. He was doing the mathematics now of how much he should set aside for the new wife and if he would have to set aside money for her home groceries as well.

"I have taken up falconry," Saad announced to Huda. "I'm going to the desert this weekend to choose a good racer. Will you be needing anything? Have fun with the kids and say hi to your mom."

That Thursday Saad met with the matchmaker again and told her his desires. He wanted a woman who was tall, fair, and shapely, with a small waist. He specified that he did not want a loose sack where the pregnancy bump had been. "I do not want a skinny woman, though," he told the matchmaker. "I want curves. And I do not want her to call me or text me. I am very happily married, but I want to enjoy what is left of my youth. I already have children, so I need her to understand that I do not want to have kids." He was trying to both justify and explain his situation. Surely there were women looking for the same thing. Someone simply looking for a husband under God's light and blessing, who had enough children and would just like to have a good time.

"Women get married to settle down. You are just looking for a hit-and-run," said the matchmaker. "None of the good families will throw their daughters down a bottomless pit without a safety net. What security will you be offering?" She looked at him without smiling. He looked at her nervously, but he was beginning to get angry.

"Everyone does it. You're making me look like a bad guy here. I hear about royals doing it all the time. You're making it sound like I'm a villain."

The guilt was setting in, and he began to feel perspiration on his forehead.

"Would you marry off your daughter to such a man?" asked the matchmaker. "Someone who is publicly uncommitted to a woman, who comes and goes as he pleases?"

She was testing him. He decided that she probably did not have any brides or wanted a higher commission than he was willing to pay. She was greedy. She probably wanted more gifts and money, and he was beginning to think that he did not get her enough groceries. He wiped his face with a handkerchief and continued his mini-battle. It did hurt to think that something like this could ever happen to his daughter, who was four. She was his dear little angel, and much more of a blessing than the troublesome boys. She was always happy with whatever he brought home, and the boys were never satisfied.

He continued to discuss, defend, and explain his situation to the matchmaker, how he would be a good husband, even if only over the weekends. With that, they parted. The matchmaker promised to keep her eyes open for a bride that suited his description. He was hesitant and almost forlorn; he felt like he had already proposed and been refused.

He pictured the Filipina barista at the coffee shop he sometimes visited in Bahrain. She always smiled at him and told him about the fruits in her country and how delicious they were. Was that a veiled hint? She was beautiful and maybe even interested in dating him, but he was too shy to ask. Besides, it was just a weekend trip that he took every few weeks to Bahrain. She probably was a good Catholic, too. If only he could get her to convert. She might be an option if the matchmaker did not do her job.

He continued going to the desert, not only to establish an alibi, but because he actually had begun to enjoy the falcon trips and gatherings with his friends. He had trained falcons in his youth, and it all came back to him quickly. He even brought his children once, and they enjoyed it very much. Huda was upset that the boys had come home with scratches, looking like they had been hit by a tumbleweed twirling across the desert. They had sand on their faces and bodies and even in their ears. "They will have to take a shower every day for a week to get all of the sand off them," she complained.

Saad turned a deaf ear. The kids had a fabulous time with Dad, which was something Huda was always complaining that he did not do enough about. Now that he had, she plucked the harp of discontent, saying that the kids were her business alone, that he was not a good example, and something about being irresponsible and immature. He held his tongue and thought about how most of his salary went to the house, schools, and vacations, leaving almost nothing for himself. His only leisure was napping and visiting his friends in their *majlis*, where they would smoke, chat, gossip, and eat. He began to wish even more that he had something for himself—his part-time wife.

A few weeks later, while he was filing paperwork at the office, the matchmaker called. "I think I have someone," she said. "She is a few years younger than you are and fits your physical requirements perfectly."

"What are her circumstances?"

"She is a widow. She has a home, but no source of income. Her parents are dead, and her remaining family cannot assist her. She has no children. She recently had a hysterectomy, so no children in the future, either. She wants someone for financial support who can satisfy her physical needs as well. She is lonely and fresh on my list of applicants."

Finally, he thought. Tailor-designed. He could not have asked for a better fit. He held his breath; the excitement was coursing through his veins. "How often would she expect me to visit?"

"Actually, that is entirely up to you. I would say twice a week is average," the matchmaker said, drawing out the word "average." Saad knew she was making a joke.

"Can she refuse me?" He trembled. His ego had been rocked by the delay in getting a response, and even his friends had gone quiet about finding him someone. All they could come up with were old, shriveled women or young gold-diggers who wanted an arm, a leg, and a kidney after they cleared out your life savings.

"She will not refuse you. You would be surprised. A lot of men talk about doing this, but very few go through with it. She will accept you. Just do not embarrass me. Do not dance on the wounds of other injured folks. Remember God and fear Him in these women. Remember, you have daughters."

"I will," said Saad.

"She's from Jeddah, by the way. You wanted her from a different area, and she is almost from a different region altogether. Your family will never see her, and your marriage will be safe. I will take you to see her. Remember, I take my gift firsthand when you hand over the dowry."

"Of course," said Saad.

The next day, Saad met his friends in the desert. Winter was coming, and everyone was getting ready to go traveling for hunting purposes. People enjoyed traveling to Algeria, Sudan, Iraq, Tajikistan, and Africa. Hunting was always a passion amongst men of the region, an addiction that, once acquired, was difficult to resist. The thrill of bagging a gazelle or fetching a net full of fish was something the hunter alone could appreciate and take pride in.

Ironically, the focus on the trigger and the fallen game had a peaceful, hypnotic allure all its own, one that did not include matters such as "We have to find a new maid because the old one had to leave urgently due to a death in the family" or, "Your son is in detention and you must attend a fifteen-minute meeting with the principal." He could be a caveman, and no one would judge him because he had cut his finger from a falcon struggling with a hunted pheasant. He could be a care-free child in the playground, winning as many tournaments as possible and celebrating amidst his clan.

"This week is my first race," Saad told Huda after work the next Thursday. "I will go out to the desert tonight and come back on Saturday."

Huda wished him luck. *She does not act like she will even miss me,* Saad thought to himself. *When did we become siblings and stop being husband and wife?* He was the bank, and she was the house supervisor, and that was all.

That Thursday night, the matchmaker accompanied him to meet Najwa from Jeddah. "She is the perfect candidate," the matchmaker assured him. She had seen Najwa earlier and would not stop telling him about the sweets that she had hand-made for him. She talked about it so much that Saad worried the new wife would make him fat.

Physically, Najwa was everything he had hoped for. She did not look the age she claimed; more like ten years younger, if not fifteen. She was tall, fair, and well-proportioned. Her never having had children served her figure well. She looked clean, peaceful, and sweet. She was a bit shy, but they got along well. He chatted about his hunting trips and childhood adventures, and she spoke about the books she enjoyed reading, the funny series that were being re-aired after Ramadan, and the excess of funny soaps to watch. She promised that she would cook him dinner whenever he visited. She amused him and warmed his heart. She did not ask about his wife, but he did mention in all honesty that he was happily married, although he and his wife lived like siblings. He stayed in it because of the kids. They agreed to get married in the morning in the presence of a religious sheikh. Everything was perfect.

The next day was Saad's dream come true. He did not know how long Najwa had been a widow, but however long it was, she had not forgotten how to please a man. She was an oasis, and he drank in her beauty. He could not believe his good fortune. She was caring and gentle, and he felt like a bull in her garden. He loved her cooking and thoroughly enjoyed his time with her.

Feeling guilty, Saad bought Huda a gift on the way home.

"You must have had good luck with your falcon," said Huda as she unwrapped the jeweled bracelet he brought her from the airport.

"Yes, I did," said Saad.

"Is he fast?"

"Fast, but he has stamina, too," said Saad, proud of himself. "I just need to train him better. He is young and gets carried away. You have to be a team with your beast, otherwise he turns rogue."

At the office, Saad was flush with newfound confidence. It was like the matchmaker said: A lot of guys talked about it, but how many actually did it? He felt like a newborn man. Everyone noticed the spring in his step. People who had not asked for his advice in years suddenly were stopping him in the hallway to get his opinion. They said he glowed like a prince and smiled like the sun. If he was not already married, his officemates would have guessed he was a newlywed groom.

Whenever he called Najwa, she answered. He was excited, and, as much as he tried to restrain himself, he simply could not resist the temptation of calling her too much. He felt like he was drinking from the grail of youth. It was a new addiction that replaced the first addiction. The dose was stronger, and he was complete.

He traveled to Bahrain for a meeting as usual, but this time he was full of energy. Even the barista at the coffee shop noticed his new confidence. She spoke to him at length for the first time.

"You work for the government, right?" she asked.

"Yes, I do," said Saad smiling.

"It must be good for the country to have someone in government as good and honest as you are," said the barista, handing him his change. "Back home, too many government workers are corrupt."

"Thank you," said Saad not even counting his change.

"What do you do?" the barista asked.

Saad tried to make his job sound important. "I work in planning. Without someone like me, none of those building projects would go anywhere."

The barista gave him a big smile, and he left her a larger-than-usual tip. *I might be able to have that girl*, he thought to himself. Immediately his thoughts turned to Najwa. *Ah, but there's no need now.* He had the confidence of a king.

The next time he saw Najwa was not nearly as exciting as the first. It lacked the anticipation and mystery that had existed before they met, the excitement of seeing her for the first time, and the thrill of their first contact. Najwa did not seem to put out the same effort. *Last time must have been her audition*, Saad joked to himself. Still, their time together was fantastic. Saad was more himself, and Najwa let him know she appreciated his attentiveness. They both were lonely and had found one another.

When he got home that weekend he made love to Huda as well.

"This falconry must have reawakened your youth," Huda remarked, teasingly. "Maybe you should have gone earlier."

Two women in one day. He felt like a thorough-bred, standing at stud. He thought of himself as Harun Al Rasheed, a great sultan back in time with the most beautiful women and harem of the land. Then again, he thought of Sultan Sulaiman of Turkey and his many wives and harem of exotic women. Had he wanted, he could have had more wives and his own harem in a house on the side. But that would be too much responsibility, too much drama, and the women would fight over him. No, he could not have that. Plus, he could never afford so many children and their trouble, bills, sicknesses, vaccinations and family trips. Huda and Najwa were more than enough. For now, anyway.

Saad had wondered if having a second wife would steal his affection for his original family, but it did not. He was happier and easier to be around, and everyone noticed. His children invited him to play their board games, and Huda began soliciting his opinion on household matters she had long decided for herself. He did feel pangs of guilt, but this redounded to his family's benefit as well. He was more generous to all of them and more accommodating of their wishes to make up for the stolen weekends and missed days. Their time was their time, and time away was his and Najwa's business. Everyone was happier.

The excitement of meeting Najwa waned over time, as one would expect. Not that she became less beautiful. On the contrary, Saad thought she was more beautiful than ever. She knew what to feed him, which scent he preferred, which movies he enjoyed, and which colors of flowers and dresses he found alluring. Perhaps because of their active weekends, she lost a couple of kilograms, making her figure even better. She did not stop wearing makeup or fixing her hair, either. In fact, Saad snapped photos of her makeup bottles and then bought her high-end versions of the same tones and colors, along with lipstick shades she liked. Slowly, Najwa replaced even the barista in Bahrain as his feminine ideal. She was his queen, and he, her king.

Their lovemaking was satisfying, but the youthful excitement had faded away. It was replaced by something else, an emotional bond that Saad had not expected to develop. As time passed, he grew more enamored of Najwa. He looked forward to their days as much as to their nights. One weekend they went to dinner at a nice restaurant and watched a movie on her couch. She fell asleep in his arms. The way she clung to his arm as she slept, with her head bowed and her neck exposed, left an image in his mind that recurred to him again and again. *My God,* he thought to himself, *I have fallen in love.*

She was a good woman who never spoke of her late husband, and he was too nervous to even bring him up. He was jealous of the memory that his now dear, dear rose held of her late husband. He had died in his sleep a few years earlier. She had no immediate family, and after he passed away, she became an introvert, only leaving the house when necessary. Her late husband could not have children, and, after he died, she had drifted into a depression which caused her to have lengthy periods. Doctors advised her to have her uterus removed, because this was a sign of early stage cancer of the endometrial lining, uterus, and cervix. She loved children, but was never blessed with them.

Saad was proud of his *mesyar* wife, but was content with the relationship staying secret. There was no need to ruin a perfect understanding. Maybe in the future he would bring her to Riyadh and rent an apartment for her closer to his home.

Whenever possible, he would make an excuse to leave home on Wednesday instead of on Thursday. Sometimes he returned late on Saturday night. As his friends had predicted, he discovered new ways of spending time with his beautiful new love. He spent one weekend in his friend's chalet by the beach, and another in the desert in his friend's tent. He even once took her with him to one of his friend's family gatherings, and she was just as reserved as he was.

One day he did not have to think of a new excuse; one fell into his lap, almost literally. A leaking air conditioner had weakened the roof of his office and, one Monday afternoon, it crashed through the ceiling. With the extreme summer heat, the entire office was given the week off with pay while repairs were made. It was a Godsend, and Saad seized upon his good fortune. He went home early and told Huda what had happened. "I can take a few days to go to Jordan to look for a new racer," he said. "Also, my friend has an uncle there who is thinking about selling his Land Rover. I might be able to get a great deal on it."

As usual, Huda put up no resistance; as long as the bills were paid and he was home eventually, all would be fine. In fact, she packed him a lunch to take with him. She was a good wife and mother, and Saad realized that he loved her even if he was not as attracted to her as he once had been.

Saad showered, shaved, and packed a few things for his week with Najwa. He left right after the children returned from school. "Have fun, Daddy," they said as he left.

Najwa never texted him unless he texted her first. He decided not to let her know he was coming. He felt a surprise visit would be a delightful treat for the growing love that was still in its blooming spring. He sent her one short message: *I cannot wait to see you.* A minute later, she texted him back. *I cannot wait to see you, either.*

It was dark when he reached Jeddah. Once inside Najwa's compound, he dimmed his lights so she would not see him coming. He parked in his usual parking place and tiptoed to the door. He slipped his key into the lock and quietly turned the handle before knocking his usual knock: "Honey, I'm home." He then flung the door open and shouted, "Surprise!"

A dark, bearded man sitting in front of the television in his pajamas and slippers looked up. "Who the hell are you?" he shouted.

"Who am I?" Saad shouted back. "Who are you?"

The man, a few years older than Saad, but feisty, sprang out of the chair like a wild animal. "Get out of my house!" the man roared.

For a moment, Saad thought he might have gone into the wrong apartment. *But why did the key fit?* he wondered. It was the last thought he had before the stranger hit him on the side of the head with a blunt object. Stunned, Saad collapsed to one knee. The man had a half-full water bottle in his hand and was raising it to strike another blow.

"Stop!" screamed Najwa, running in from the kitchen. "Stop! He's a friend!"

"A friend?" shouted the man.

A friend? thought Saad.

"Why does he have a key?" the fuming man demanded.

131

Saad struggled to his feet. "Because I am her husband, you idiot."

The man swung the water bottle again, but this time Saad blocked the man's wrist, and the bottle flew out of his hand.

"Get the hell out of my house," shouted the man.

His voice boomed out the open door and echoed off the apartment building on the other side of the parking lot. Najwa's neighbors already were calling the police.

"You get out," shouted Saad. "Tell him, Najwa."

The man looked at Najwa. "What is he saying?"

"Has this man hurt you?" Saad asked Najwa. "Did you hurt her?" he yelled at the man.

"Not like I'm going to hurt you," said the man, grabbing a candlestick from the sideboard behind the couch. "I'll make you bleed."

"Ahmed, stop," screamed Najwa, grabbing the man's arm.

"Do you know this man?" demanded Saad. "Well, do you?"

He looked at the two of them. Najwa was clinging to the man's arm the way she had clung to his on the couch when she was asleep. Saad's head was throbbing, but he hardly felt it. He prayed the man was her brother, but he was not sure of how to react. He just felt the adrenaline rush, his jealousy reaching a dangerous point, and his arms burning him where she held this strange man. The pain in his heart was too great. He wanted an explanation.

The police sorted out the details. Najwa was married to the other man, Ahmed. An aircraft technician, Ahmed made a good living by working weekends and holidays when airline travel was busiest. That is when Saad would visit. Ahmed was off Mondays and Tuesdays, when Saad was never around. He was her husband of many years and he could not have children. After she had her hysterectomy, her mother-in-law, whom she never liked, convinced Ahmed to take his spinster cousin as a second wife. Najwa never recovered from the insult. She demanded a divorce, but one was never granted, and Ahmed continued to live with her, although he would hardly ever see her. She considered herself divorced because according to Islam, if a husband chooses not to consummate a marriage for more than six months and does not provide for his wife and home, then she is technically a divorcee. But she must apply for the divorce and prove it before going ahead with such an audacious act.

Najwa had mischievously arranged a *mesyar* marriage with a new man to profit from and enjoy, as the man had likewise enjoyed her. Since she had married Ahmed first, she was legally bound to him, but because she had made a joke of the institution of marriage, she was arrested and taken to prison.

Najwa had her day in court. She defended herself by claiming that she had merely played the men's game of cheating on their wives and of fooling themselves into thinking that any woman would be honored to be made into a glorified prostitute. The court found her guilty of polygamy, which was punishable by imprisonment of up to two years, but her life was spared because both marriages were full of holes. Saad appeared at her trial and begged for the court's mercy on the woman who had betrayed him.

"Why are you defending her?" asked the judge.

"Because I am the injured party," said Saad. "And because . . ." His throat tightened, and he paused to take a deep breath. "And," he said at last, "because I love her."

I Sold My Kidney for Love

I LIKE MEN WHO MAKE me laugh. Adnan was hilarious and quick-witted when we met our junior year in university in Yemen. He expressed a keen interest in me, which I reciprocated. I just wanted him to know that I was looking for a serious relationship, one that would end in marriage.

Born into a working-class family, I was of average build, with shoulder-length, curly brown hair, almond eyes, and an aquiline nose. I always dressed in pastel colors because I felt that even if I were to have a bad day, the colors would subdue any negativity and bring out the peace within me. I excelled in university and would assist students in help session classes where my feelings toward Adnan, my fellow student, blossomed. His magnetism and kindness were visible and unforgettable. I enjoyed sitting next to him as much as I enjoyed his discussions in class amongst his peers. We both created reasons to speak or work together, and, surely enough, a love was kindled.

I insisted to this fellow Yemeni who understood our traditions that the marriage would have to be formally arranged if he insisted on controlling my life, my friends, my attire, and my lifestyle. He was as attentive as he was funny. His uncle came to our house to propose and formally take permission to get us engaged. It was agreed that we were to be married after university, hopefully. Money is always everyone's problem when considering tying the knot. Circumstances are always complicated, especially for two young adults who are each trying to create their own destiny. Yet I believed in Adnan, and a future with him was my ultimate dream. He would be my happy ending, and I would do my utmost to make it work.

One day, I was out shopping with my cousin for her engagement and we bumped into a relative of her fiancé. Surprisingly, it was Adnan's uncle—the same one I had met! I was shocked and tried to understand the relation. Since Adnan was of a Southern tribe and I was of a Northern tribe, I was astonished that both my and my friend's fiancés were related, and both were from this Southern tribe. The uncle's first name was the same as it had been introduced to me, but his second name was not. Questions were raised, and I demanded answers. The air was tense, and I was confused. I did not want to wait, and I was getting angry. Feeling cheated is a rage that escalates like an erupting volcano. The stories of staged proposals and men who get away with breaking girls' hearts raced through my mind. I was drowning in doubt as I recalled long conversations where Adnan would complain bitterly of how poor he was and how difficult it would be to afford the wedding, let alone the marriage and children that, God willing, would follow.

I confronted Adnan on the university campus and demanded a formal explanation. Why did he bring in a stranger to pretend to be his uncle and trick me into thinking that he was serious about our relationship? Why did he lie to me? I needed to understand the situation or end it. I set off a firework of inquiries as this appeared to be dishonesty in its plainest form and function—a ruse to lure me into a relationship with someone who seemed to be looking for a fling, not a marriage. Was he just looking to legitimize our relationship because he knew very well that I would refuse a short-term dating scheme? I was in it for marriage, as was the norm for respectable girls in our tribes and country. Men and women are not allowed or approved of to be friends and dating without a proper proposal.

Adnan was apologetic and tried to fix the broken trust. He explained how his family was not educated and would never agree to him marrying a liberal woman; this is why he had asked a friend to pose as his uncle. By liberal, he was referring to my modest self, because I do not wear a hijab, I went to a mixed university, and conversed, albeit conservatively, with my fellow colleagues or coworkers regardless of their gender. I would not be comfortable in his culture, traditions, and accepted norms. All of this being said, Adnan said he was different from the rest of his family and did not care what they thought. His long-term plan was to earn a high enough salary to afford independent housing from his family, pay for a decent wedding and dowry, and to support us both.

I did not speak to him and did not answer his calls for weeks. He told me he loved me and that he would go the distance. I do not know if I chose to believe his sincerity and his desperate tears, or if I simply could not picture any other man besides him in my life. My grandmother used to say "we get who we dream of in heaven," and to me, he was my prince in heaven. I knew that I loved him so very much, beyond common sense or reason. I would go to sleep picturing his face next to mine on my pillow and would sometimes wake, crying from a dream in which he would die, and that would leave me emotionally traumatized.

Eventually, we came back together, and Adnan promised me that he would propose properly after graduating. I forgave him and loved him more after that, and he was more attentive to me as well, stating that the time and punishment he had faced was enough to kill a grown man. A few months later, I graduated as an accountant and began taking CPA courses to improve my chances of getting a job.

Adnan graduated with me, but his calls and visits soon began to dwindle. I began to wonder why and faced him with my fears. He broke down when I saw him, telling me that he could not afford to get married and that he was ashamed to speak to me. Additionally, he faced trouble with his family as they had recently lost their car to torching during one of the recent strikes in Yemen.

I was constantly thinking of ways to be able to aid my Adnan in affording our dream. I worked part time as a tutor after my full-time job, as exhausting as it was, but the savings were never enough. Teaching children and college students is mentally taxing, especially after maintaining the business and private tax accounts of those who needed me. Then one day we were joking about ways of making money, and Adnan casually said, "Selling a kidney or going into slavery are the only options I have left to be with you."

The desperate idea was born.

I laughed it off at first, but then I began toying with it. It involved risk, but so does love. It involved danger, but I was brave. I had exhausted all other possible solutions to be with the man I wanted to have a family with and grow old with. He was the love of my life, and I, his. We would be together finally; all else seemed distant and unimportant.

I began to dig into the procedure. When I first discussed it with Adnan, he told me that I was barking mad and that many have died after donating a kidney because the body simply cannot handle it. He could not do it due to the physical demands of his job, but he did not know of any other way for us to be married. I said that if I had to be the man in the relationship, I would buck up and do it. He never thought that I would go through with it, and yet he never stopped me from discussing my plans with what we would do when I received the payment for my kidney. I was brave, rash, and headstrong. I decided that this was the fastest way to rectify my situation and hasten my happy ending with my prince.

Adnan showered me with love after I made that deci-sion for our relationship, but I knew that the procedure needed to happen quickly in order for the marriage to occur amidst our family differences.

I went to the hospital with my passport and registered as someone willing to donate my kidney for a price. With trembling hands I signed the consent form that began, "I consent to sell/donate my kidney." The date for the surgery was set in one week. There were many people on dialysis who were dying, slowly withering, or delaying their death and waiting for a savior, a spare kidney. It dawned on me that should my remaining kidney fail or falter, I would be in the same line, lying in bed for hours every week. The urea would rise in my body, and I would suffer, but I was strong and had never suffered from any illnesses so I hoped it would never come to that.

I began to pray harder and deeper after signing away my spare kidney. I was afraid of death. I was afraid of everything around me, but love pushed me forward. I did not inform my family, as they would surely try to stop me. I entered the operating theater one week later, and Adnan stood there holding my hand as I drifted into a deep sleep. Hours later, I woke up dizzy and drowsy. It was done. I did not feel a thing.

My kidney was sold to a fifty-three-year-old butcher. He had gone to the Philippines to buy a kidney but after his surgery, his body had rejected it. He returned home to Yemen, thinking it might be a better idea to obtain a local kidney because it might adjust better. He was a good man, feeding many poor families with his charity. He would send extra meat for stew to the orphans so they would have at least one decent meal per day. I felt that by giving my kidney to a deserving man, I would be doing something for the greater good. That helped calm me down in the midst of my reckless storm of thoughts.

His family came to see me and give me the check. They called me their daughter, and his grandchildren kissed my hands and called me their sister. It was a beautiful feeling to be able to give life to someone so loved. I imagined them as mine and Adnan's grandchildren one day.

Adnan visited me in the hospital but he said he was afraid of the sick and dying and felt overwhelmed. He cried like a baby, and I was too weak to calm him. I gave him the check, and he began speaking of how this was going to be our new start, our home, and that he would spend his life making it up to me.

After he left that day, I suffered from nightmares. I was hoping I would be able to leave the hospital that night, but I fell ill with a fever and had to stay. I returned home the next day, giving my family the excuse that I had fallen sick with all the exhaustion of teaching classes to children and adults and had spent the night with a friend. I remained bedridden for two weeks. Adnan never called me, and I was either asleep or feverish so could not go inquiring after him. I did not have credit on my phone and my body was battling to survive with one kidney. My family thought I was dying. I never told them the real reason I was sick for fear that they would hate Adnan or think of how desperate, crazy, and obsessed I was about being with him.

When I was strong enough, I went to his home and knocked at his glass door. He lived with his parents and four brothers, and I was hoping his parents would not attend to the door. I wanted to know where the man I risked my life for was. Why did he not call, send after me, or visit me?

Why didn't he at least send a friend or bring his family to propose properly? There were no excuses—absolutely none—for his delay. I thought that maybe he wanted to go and buy the ring, but we had already chosen our rings. We had named our pets, our children, and even grandchildren, if our children would let us. We had an understanding, but one I did not understand anymore. I was weak and frail and I wanted him to take care of me. I felt the tears welling up, but I did not want to cry before learning where he had been all this time and why he was not with me.

A young lady opened the door. She was short and plump with a round nose and round eyes. She was very fair and had a beauty spot on her upper lip. She had her hair in a turban, so I wasn't sure if she was the part-time maid or his cousin over helping his mother in the kitchen, as obviously she was comfortably dressed to be a part of the household. I was dressed in a long white skirt and a light jacket, as I was always cold. Conversely, she was dressed in every color of the rainbow and looked at me like I was either a spy or a saleswoman trying to force her to buy my chutney or sweets.

"Can I please see Adnan?" I asked reluctantly and shyly.

"Who are you to ask about my husband?" she snapped.

"I . . . er . . . What do you mean? When?" It was hard. Harder than losing a kidney and waking up dead in a grave. I trembled and leaned on the wall. "Please. Gently. I need to understand. Where is Adnan?"

I was in a shock so backbreaking I felt it slam my head, body, and soul with the force of a boulder crashing down a mountain. I was in shock. The ramifications were too much, and I slowly lost control of my balance and fainted.

The neighbors were there to witness the incident. The woman slammed the door, and I could hear yelling and swearing inside. The neighbors took me in, and I could still hear a distant yelling over the phone as it seemed she was calling both her family and my Adnan to better understand the situation. His neighbors explained to me that Adnan had received an offer to work abroad and the employer had sent him the salary a month in advance. He had used the money to marry his cousin.

I was taken for a fool. There was no employer; Adnan had used my kidney money to marry his cousin. He had been engaged to her since his first year in university, and his family disapproved of women who were liberal like me, who studied and worked with men. They never would have accepted me. He had led me to believe that he was serious about me and that all would be all right in the end. Instead, he took my money and sold my love.

Voodoo in New York

THE LANDLINE PHONE ON the marble pedestal rang midmorning. Maryam, pregnant with her first child, gave the phone a suspicious look. She had asked her husband, Khalifa, to add caller ID to their account. Busy with his PhD studies in urban design and architecture in the Middle East at New York University, he had put off the request for a couple of weeks. Exasperated, Maryam had called the phone company herself and ordered the service, but was told it would take a few days to activate.

The phone rang again. It was not Khalifa; he would have called her on her mobile. It could be her mother calling from abroad, or it could be someone trying to reach Khalifa about his work. It could be something about their apartment building, or a bill, or clothing ready to be picked up from the cleaners. It might even be one of the new friends she had made in yoga class. Maryam decided to answer. Why is movement such a feat when you are pregnant?

It was him. The foreigner.

"I must speak to you. Please. I don't want to frighten you, but . . ."

Maryam took a deep breath the way she learned in yoga class. Breathe in, breathe out, ever so slowly and completely. In a couple of days she would have caller ID and would never have to hear that voice again.

The caller spoke English with an accent that seemed to Maryam to be from the Arabian Gulf. She recognized those accents. A hushed voice that sounded husky and rough, hard-edged. Or maybe that was his personality. When a woman is pregnant, she is too tired to analyze. Quietly end it—no discussion, no quarrels, no explanations. Just hang up.

She had thought that maybe he was one of those scammers who made money by keeping you on the line, but then she was not dialing out. He was dialing in, so there should not be a charge on her bill. Still, maybe there was a way to secretly reverse the charges. There were technology wizards all over the world who would rather make easy money off of hardworking people than to apply their skills to something worthwhile. Where were the typical honest and hardworking early birds who worked 9-to-5 jobs, as opposed to hackers, swindlers and quacks? Where were the people who wanted to make the world a better place for the next generation?

"I need to speak to you," he whispered. "Are you alone?" He sounded serious and the news he wanted to share, urgent. Maryam paused for a few seconds and then put the phone down quietly.

Whatever he had to say was going to raise her blood pressure, and she was still a few weeks away from her delivery date. She was not in any hurry to nurse a premature baby. She had read that the longer the baby gestates, the better its health and the larger its size at birth.

She patted her growing baby bump. The man had sounded menacing. She was not frightened for herself; she was afraid for her baby. They call it adrenaline, the fight-or-flight hormone: If you are strong enough, you fight. If you are weaker, you take flight. She felt her pulse begin to slowly rise from the urgency in his tone and felt a cloud of bad news descending around her. She did not even want to know whatever it was that she should avoid. Sometimes the stress preceding a warning is enough to give you an early delivery, and she was not ready to deliver yet. Khalifa was not due home for at least another two hours.

It did not seem realistic to think that anything could touch her in her home, a fifty-second-floor apartment on the Upper East Side of New York City. She had moved there with her new husband a year earlier. It was an arranged marriage that had gone well, but happiness always requires persistence. After all, relationships are a continuous job of making them work once one ails or gives up and the other runs on the memory of the good times.

When she looked out the window, she felt like she was at the top of the world, seeing everything from a new, lofty perspective. As she looked down at the streets, she at once felt the eccentricity of the magnificent city that seemed to embrace her—a sense of promise of a new life that beckoned in the city the world affectionately calls The Big Apple.

New York was even bigger and better than she had pictured. Movies could not capture the fresh, crisp breeze when you went for a brisk walk in the park or the squirrel that rushed past you and up a mighty tree that looked older than your grandparents. The feeling of snow delicately falling on your hands and melting instantly. The gentle crushing of snow and slush beneath your feet. How you could not wear sandals or fashionable heels in the winter: No one could teach you things like these, or even begin to explain them. Only time and experience revealed the atmosphere of the buzzing city that never sleeps.

Maryam loved how she could latch on to her husband as they walked for warmth and exaggerated intimacy and further enjoyed that he would not view it as needy or choking him. She would smile until her cheeks blushed at the secret delight that he never knew; walking arm-in-arm was her stolen pleasure. It was part of American culture, she thought, and she was learning, drinking up what she enjoyed and helping herself to whatever suited her in her new lifestyle.

She knew about towers, but the towers of New York were mountains that housed people from six continents. Tens of thousands of people lived and worked in the buildings, and every day she would see new faces in her block. The daily adventure of rediscovering the same path with new faces was exciting, although she sometimes missed the familiarity of seeing the same faces every day. There was no time or place to be racist or biased against any one religion or color or political belief, because New York was too much of a melting pot for anyone to be deemed odd or out of place.

She became friends with The Halal Guys, a caravan of healthy Arab fast food located on every other block that sold the best shawarma in the city. It was homey, it really was. The staff would acknowledge her and give her a free helping of extra dressing, telling her New York would grow on her eventually. She prayed that it would be soon, because she was still trying to find her niche, her familiar spots, and her comfort zone in The Big Apple. The simple and unique comfort of walking anywhere you wanted to get whatever you needed was liberating. People were unaffected by your appearance regardless of whether you were smartly dressed or barely decorated. There was a place and time for everyone, and everyone had his or her own niche and home base. There was no possible way to feel lonely, or was there? The city was always alive, always busy. People were always ready to chat for ten seconds and then casually walk away. Comments like "How many months are you along?" and "Where about are you from?" were as common as "How are you?" and "Have a nice day."

And yet, as the weeks passed, the novelty had started to wear off, and Maryam was left feeling empty and dissatisfied. She was unable to find in her neighborhood any woman with similar circumstances as hers who was available to meet at convenient times. Khalifa was preoccupied with his studies at NYU and his diplomat job at the embassy, spending most of the day with important guests and diplomats. By the time he came home in the evenings, he was spent.

Maryam decided she would try to make friends, so she signed up to take some English courses at a nearby community college. This did not turn out as well as she had hoped. Most of the people in the class were busy—business people who had been transferred to New York and needed to learn the language fast, foreign students trying to improve their English-language skills in time to take exams and write papers, and immigrants in service positions trying to advance their careers. There was no one like her, a homemaker just trying to get along in this strange country and to make a new friend by joining an English class. Her classmates were all racing to be somewhere, build an empire, discover something, or conquer a mountain, and she just wanted a teatime playmate. Her ambitions were too simple to be voiced, so she simply worked on her language skills and went home.

Khalifa noticed Maryam was tired and asked how he could help. She told him about her unsuccessful attempts at making friends and how she had just given up.

"I'm tired of staring out the window day in and day out. I don't mean to sound bothersome, but you're always at work or running errands, and I'm tired of shopping alone, watching TV alone, and eating alone."

She stopped talking when she noticed his helpless look, expecting his response to be guilt-ridden with no solution. She lost the purpose of finishing her sentence somewhere between complaining and knowing his doomed response. Her voice choked as tears welled up in her big brown eyes.

Khalifa held her for a few minutes quietly. He did not know what his lonely wife wanted. He came home every evening longing for rest, but besides the never-ending troubles at work, there now was a calamity at home. His safe haven was falling to pieces. Maryam mumbled something he could neither hear nor understand.

"Please don't cry," he said. His forehead and eyebrows knotted as he searched her face for answers. "Let's go out now. Er, wait, it's too late. I was going to take you shopping." That always made her happy, but New York was not Arabia, where shops and bazaars were open from morning till late night.

"Honey, I have a married friend. I'm sure you'd like to meet his wife—she could be your friend."

To cheer Maryam up, Khalifa introduced her to his friend's wife, Maha, who was also Arab. Same customs, culture, habits, language and accent—this was all Khalifa knew about her, and that she was from a rich family and married to one of Khalifa's colleagues at work. In short, Maha belonged to the same social circle as Maryam, only came from a different Arab state.

A petite bronze but a stone overweight, Maha was attractive for her age, with a pretty face and round features; tiny, fat hands with long, painted nails with crystals glued onto them; and thick, dark hair. She was very energetic and just a few years older than Maryam. She spoke Maryam's dialect, and it was exciting to trade stories about life where Maryam had grown up. But Maha also was somewhat materialistic and liberal in her actions. Usually, she was quiet and well-mannered, but then she would suddenly complain bitterly about her husband's friends, whom she referred to as "parasites." Maha felt her husband spent too much time and money on his opportunistic friends, to his disadvantage and hers. He received his job because of his status and was listed as a student, but he attended neither work nor school, except when absolutely necessary.

Other things about her new friend also bothered Maryam—small, trivial things, but they all added up to an unpleasant picture that left her feeling disconcerted. Maha had an exaggerated number of servants in her Manhattan penthouse, yet somehow the home was always messy. Perhaps it was crowded with too many useless servants loitering around. Other things just seemed out of sync. She had strung up glittery foil decorations at the entrance of the penthouse; wine and coffee stains appeared on her expensive sofas; and an electronic snowman with lights was placed in front of the fireplace in the middle of May. The house was dirty, and Maryam felt uncomfortable sitting on the chairs without dusting cigarette ashes off of them and removing random rubbish like school papers or official documents that were scattered about. The fridge contained nothing but fast-food leftovers and bottles of alcohol. Maha had a cinema room with a 120-inch screen, but inside the room the stench of cigarettes and alcohol was suffocating. The light-colored carpets were flecked with cigarette ashes, as if no one had ever vacuumed. Whenever Maryam visited, she could not wait to leave.

Maryam invited her friend to go grocery shopping, to take a stroll in the park, or to go to the movies, but Maha had no interest in entertainment, shopping, or even visiting salons.

Maryam took great pride in the appearance of her home. She decorated it herself, showing a flair for design by mixing exquisite Persian carpets with Greek pedestals and statues that she bought on eBay. She created an interior with a positive vibe, making it as nurturing as possible to a husband who had to concentrate on his studies when he came home. She had spent her first days studying colors, interior design magazines, and feng shui, piecing together her broken English to better understand what the text along with the pictures meant. She was content with the result and rested comfortably in her humble nest high in the tower.

Obtaining a doctorate was Khalifa's priority. He made it clear he wanted to finish his studies before having children, and he had no desire for an active social life. Maryam supported his decision, and was happy about it and proud of her husband's ambition. She liked to think of their time together in New York as a sort of extended honeymoon. It was a prolonged time to allow them to grow on each other and cement their relationship, independent of the opinions of others.

Maha, on the other hand, was trying hard to get pregnant in the hopes that if she did her husband, who loved children, would pay more attention to her. Maha was very secretive about her husband and spoke very little about him, other than the occasional negative remarks. Still, she craved his attention.

When Maha visited Maryam's apartment, she would always compare their houses, their husbands, their clothing, and other things. Maha gave the impression that she was entitled to a better home, husband, education, and status in life than Maryam. Maryam felt she was made to feel inferior, and green envy oozed whenever Maha spoke. Narcissistic and arrogantly rude, even bordering on slightly offensive, Maha was not in the slightest bit worried about how Maryam would react to her brash comments. Maryam dismissed it, thinking that Maha was probably going through a rough patch with her husband or that the pregnancy-inducing hormones she was taking were making her moody and snappy. Such are the things that dire circumstances force you into accepting so as not to suffer alone.

Some of Maha's bragging might have been true, but Maryam believed that her friend had a drinking problem. Maryam was so lonesome that she never mentioned her suspicions to Khalifa, who would surely disapprove. She feared he would cut off her connection to her only Gulf Arab friend. Sometimes when they met in the morning, Maha's eyes would be so rimmed with red that even her lids looked sensitive and pink, with the blue, hair-like capillaries evident under her delicate, fair skin. Her breath would be a poisonous stench that even chewing on a few sticks of gum would not clear. Her midnight texts and calls sometimes made no sense at all, leaving Maryam slightly confused and raising the distinct possibility that her friend was a typical drunk.

Khalifa confirmed Maryam's suspicions when he witnessed Maha in a drunken brawl at the mezzanine bar balcony in the Plaza Hotel where he was meeting with some students. He witnessed the scene and told his wife not to associate with Maha anymore.

"They had to drag her out; it was embarrassing to witness," said Khalifa. "Her husband was with us earlier. He would never show his face again if he had seen his wife escorted out by force."

Khalifa knitted his eyebrows, recalling the experience. "Arabs can't drink. And when they do, they make a spectacle of themselves. Men and women, both. You know, they say Native Americans are the same; their blood can't handle the alcohol. One drink and they're on fire."

★　★　★

Khalifa was working on one of his three-dimensional architectural renderings. As he was cutting one of his thin pressed cardboard planks for the stairs of his architectural creation, the knife slipped, and he cut himself. Maryam passed him a tissue with which he dabbed the tip of his finger. The bleeding stopped and he went back to work. He enjoyed it, and Maryam enjoyed watching him construct buildings, the dancing cardboard walls encapsulating chambers that looked like minimalist theatrical

154

sets from outer space. She admired his long lashes and arched eyebrows as he focused on bringing the walls together.

Khalifa was tall, fit, and somewhat bookish looking, perhaps because of his black-rimmed glasses. He was shy but hardworking; focused, but on occasion socially autistic. His hair was overgrown, so he just began tying it back, not to affect a hippie style, but because he did not notice or care enough to visit the barber. He dressed in plain blue jeans and tartans every day, on school days and off days alike—never fancy, but practical and ready to help. Good old Kali, always dependable. He would spend all night slicing and organizing the geometric parts of his paper buildings. Maryam even learned to cut and shave the cardboard planks so she could work with him on his creations. They spent numerous hours dissecting paper, creating one masterpiece after another.

With the changing of the seasons and times, Maryam's English improved. She began to understand the language on the street, read posters and understand them, and enjoy her conversations with total strangers in stores, on the street, or when feeding the ducks at the park. Times were warming as the season was cooling and the leaves began to turn color. During the most colorful period of the year, people were whimsically dressed and walked with an extra jump in their step, almost like they were dancing. Being an Arab, Maryam attributed the lively behavior to the unfamiliar cold, but she enjoyed how it made her want to laugh more readily. Her lost friend Maha was quietly replaced by the world of New York and Maryam's eventual integration into American society, which she learned was not difficult once you absorbed the norms, food, and eccentricities, and knew when to avoid and when to entertain them.

As disappointed as Maryam was to lose a friend who shared her common background, no one misses a negative sloth for long. This was especially true because soon after breaking off contact with Maha, Maryam found out that she was pregnant with an unplanned baby. It was uncalculated in the equation of their current life, apartment, and travel plans, and Khalifa, who was so intent on finishing his studies uninterrupted, was reserved about the news. He made a list of how the small bundle of diapers was going to wreak havoc on their home: the need for his own room, his sleeping timings, emergency contacts, baby sitters, and a midwife, versus travel plans and exam schedules. Maryam smiled and quietly agreed that disaster was about to strike, but what to do? Inwardly, she began to get nervous at the prospect of increased responsibilities just as she was beginning to settle into her new home.

Once Khalifa had the opportunity to digest the news and reorganize his life plans, he was delighted and told his family. Who could say no to a bundle of joy? Soon afterwards, everything began to fall into place. Maryam enjoyed fussing over the baby's room and acquiring books, toys, and clothes. She took up yoga and would rise at dawn and perform sun salutations for an hour daily. Even Maryam's facility with the English language and accent improved after joining a pregnant moms group. Her balcony garden on her fifty-second-floor apartment bloomed. She spent hours with her greenery and roses, considering it her personal oasis in the concrete jungle.

However, even in paradise, the proverbial evil snake lurked.

This was about the time that Maryam received the first phone call from the man overseas. All he would say was: "I need to speak to you." She did not know how he got her number, but it could have been just a random dial. What was strange was that she also began to receive emails from him. *Please answer my phone calls*, the stranger wrote. *I need to speak with you. It's an urgent matter.* Perhaps it was not all that strange that he had obtained her email address. In today's world, people can gather all kinds of information about you from electronic records. Perhaps he had hacked into her Facebook account or another online account that had her personal information. Regardless, the man was harassing her. With her pregnancy nearing its third term, Maryam grew restless and angry at the man's persistence.

As usual, Maryam did not reply to the email. Instead, when Khalifa came home from the embassy, Maryam told him about it and the strange phone calls. He read the emails and made a few calls to friends. A technology expert from the embassy came over that evening and examined

Maryam's computer and phone records. The stalker, whoever he was, had not done much to conceal his identity. A few clicks and keystrokes later, Khalifa's friend had pinpointed the source. The calls and emails were coming from Kuwait. A little more sleuthing, and they had a name to go with the email address. The next morning, Khalifa made a call to the Kuwaiti police from the embassy. It was not official business, but the police did not need to know that. He was a diplomat from the embassy in the United States, and that was enough said.

The police picked up the mysterious caller and brought him in for questioning. The man denied having any financial or indecent motives. He told a tale so fantastic that the police had no choice but to believe him.

He said he was the ex-lover of Maryam's former friend, Maha. She had sent him a package with instructions that it be delivered to a man at a certain address, saying it was a donation for charity. He took the package to the address but was startled to find it was a graveyard. Taken aback, he felt that there was more to the box than mere charity. Worried that it might contain drugs or contraband, the Kuwaiti man returned home and opened the box in the privacy of his own home. He was surprised to find a woman's personal articles: a silk bra and panties and a few strands of long dark hair, tied at one end with a rubber band. It was obvious that the items were not for charity. They were for a spell to be cast on their original owner. Tales of witchcraft were commonplace, and it was well known that personal articles could be used to cast an unbreakable and life-ruining spell on the person to whom the objects had once belonged.

Satisfied that he was not engaging in a prosecutable offense, the Kuwaiti left the items at home and headed to the rundown house at the graveyard with an empty package. He wanted to see who was meant to receive the woman's personal items. He passed through a broken gate with peeling paint, the ground beneath it a rusty rain color. He knocked at a door with peeling wooden planks, wondering why people involved in the magic trade tended to live in such shabby surroundings. It seemed like a curse in and of itself to possess magical powers that left you living like a starving beggar.

The man who answered looked just as the Kuwaiti imagined a warlock would: old, short, dark olive skin, missing teeth and black gums, dark circles under his eyes, and protruding eyeballs, one of which was clouded with cataracts. The man, a Yemeni, accepted the empty package, saying he had expected it a day earlier. The Kuwaiti told the police that he did not know if the caretaker had seen him the night before when he had driven by, or if he had the power of remote seeing. It did not matter. He handed the man the package and left.

That night and for many nights afterwards, the Kuwaiti had nightmares about the Yemeni caretaker with the bulging eyes and missing teeth. He decided he had to warn whomever it was that the sorcerer was getting paid to hurt. He called Maha and as casually as possible inquired who the articles in the package had belonged to. Angry that

Maryam had cut off all contact with her and jealous of her pregnancy, Maha did not try to hide who was the object of her wrath. She confided everything in her ex-lover. She told the Kuwaiti that she thought her no-good husband had taken an interest in her young, attractive friend so she decided to damage her however she could. The magic she had requested was the kind that would cause madness, illness, or suicide, as most black spells are requested to do. In her demented plan, once Maryam was at the point of death, Maha would come to her aid. Pretending to be a healer, she would have the Yemeni remove the curse and restore her to health. She would be the savior of her ailing friend.

People close to Maryam had played a part in Maha's evil plot. Maryam's maid had accepted a bribe to let her into the apartment, allowing the theft of her underwear. Maryam's hairdresser was paid to save a few strands of her hair secretly. Maha had told the hairdresser that she wanted to keep it as a keepsake; the Canadian hairdresser did not know anything about voodoo concoctions.

The Kuwaiti had broken off his relationship with Maha because of her bad temper, especially when she drank, but he never imagined that she could do something as hurtful and cruel as this. As she described the details of her plan, he realized that she was a mad, bitter woman with too much free time to spend being vindictive. Not knowing what she or her Yemeni accomplice were capable of, he feared for his life, hence his secrecy in identifying himself to Maryam.

Black magic was rare, but its negative effects could not be denied: homes wrecked, babies lost, handicaps suffered, and misfortunes galore intended to injure the victim. Even if they did not die, they would live maimed, damaged, and broken.

The police paid a visit to the Yemeni sorcerer, who by sixth or common sense realized something was wrong when he saw the box was empty. He already had fled his dilapidated lair. Whether he tried to cast a spell or not could never be determined, but no black magic ever struck Maryam.

News of the Kuwaiti lover eventually reached Maha's rich husband, who already had divorced Maha some months earlier. Her temper had escalated in their last months together. She had attacked him physically and set a small fire in their apartment. Her husband had pulled down a curtain and stamped out the fire before it spread, but the alarms had gone off and the police and fire department came. Maha tried to explain that the curtain caught fire from a lamp, and she went to fetch a wet towel to put it out. It was clear that the fire was no accident, and Maha was arrested on suspicion of arson. After verbally abusing the police officers, she was taken to a mental hospital for observation. That is when Maha's husband stopped putting any effort into the marriage.

As for Maryam, she views the world from her apartment a little differently now, filled with the warmth of her loving family. She works part time in an English program for foreign speakers. Khalifa is still pursuing his PhD at his well-organized pace and is happy walking his healthy baby boy Zayed as he shoots pictures of skyscrapers around the city. And the landline phone on the marble pedestal has finally stopped ringing.

Raped for a Living

VIOLETA'S MOTHER HAD A failing kidney and her father had lost his sight due to diabetes. She had applied for jobs in Manila, but the pay was not enough to put her younger siblings through college, which she desperately wanted to do. A better life—that was all she wanted. One where she and her family could eat ice cream every weekend, instead of once a year. One where her father could have access to insulin on a daily basis and could keep whatever he had left of his fingers and sight.

America, Europe, and Canada were overseas dreams. The salaries there were higher, the living standards were better, and employees almost always got paid on time. Who knew—she might even have her family join her in Los Angeles, pick up French while in Paris, or share a small studio with her family in New York. She had everything figured out. She would economize and work hard to prove her worth. She would advance, because these modern countries would appreciate a smart, educated, hardworking woman.

Violeta was twenty-six years old, five feet, five inches tall and of a slender build, though she had gained a bit of weight when she stopped working on the family farm.

She had a degree in hotel management and was looking to be a receptionist in a five-star hotel in a rich
country. She had long hair, large eyes, and spoke Spanish
as well as Tagalog and English due to her grandparents'
Spanish ancestry. Her family owned land, which was
an asset, but did not have enough able hands to turn
the soil and plant, tend, and harvest the crops. Farming
was a constant struggle that was regularly interrupted
by monsoons, floods, crippling pesticide costs, taxes,
and theft. The local loan shark charged exorbitant rates,
triggering a domino effect: By the time one loan was
paid, another was needed—a never-ending, unfair, and
vicious circle.

Violeta was the breadwinner in her family and wanted
very much to get married to her fiancé, Lucas Fernandez.
They had been together since high school and both
supported their families, but had backbreaking responsibilities. Lucas left the Philippines for a job in Azerbaijan
as a hotel florist, making the arrangements for the lobbies,
meeting rooms, and exclusive suites. He hoped that after
a few years he would return to the Philippines and work
at a similar caliber hotel in Manila. He sent Violeta emails
full of promises and pretty pictures of clean streets, fashionably dressed people, and flower centerpieces he had
created. Lucas was creative with his flowers, and Violeta
was especially proud of his boldest creations such as the
arrangement he made for a hotel that featured clutches of
white lilies bound with tiny vines to blood red carnations.
He would send her pictures of bridal bouquets every few

days, asking her which one she would want to carry for her wedding.

As the money from the farm began to run out, Violeta thought it best to attempt to work in these golden countries and finally use her degree. Anything seemed better than starving to death amidst the mud with a sick family and dying dreams all around her. Hard times called for hard decisions, and so she applied everywhere for a job. Many offices required that she pay an upfront fee of 50,000 pesos to receive a passport and a guarantee of a job. It was a lot of money, equivalent to the price of a plot of land in her province in the Philippines.

In a final battle against encroaching poverty, Violeta visited a pawnshop with the only thing of value that she had left: the deed to the land that belonged to her grandparents before her, the land that had fed them and given them a roof during monsoons. The pawnbroker's eyes lit up as he took the deed from Violeta's hands and read it in the bluish glare of the fluorescent lamp that hung over the cash register. He glanced at Violeta, as if to see how determined she would be to pay back the loan, then carefully counted out the money she needed for her passport; a down payment to guarantee her loyalty and seriousness about traveling to work abroad. A smile crept over his lips as Violeta signed the loan agreement. *He thinks the land will be his,* Violeta thought, *but I will pay this back in time to keep it.*

After paying the employment agency, Violeta had a little extra money left, which she left behind with her siblings, all under the age of eighteen. Sibila, seventeen, wanted to be a fashion designer, but Violeta wanted her to go into nursing, where the pay was better. The twins, Anthon and Antonella, fifteen, wanted to be actors and singers, but Violeta wanted them to be an architect and civil engineer so they could work together as they were both good at drawing and quick in math. Maria Mercedes, the doe-eyed thirteen-year-old, towered for her young age and aspired to be a model. Violeta was the mother figure in the house and she would sometimes find herself crying in desperation at how dreamy and unaware her brood was about their poverty. Her father ate less and less because he thought that he was leaving food to sustain his children. His condition required that he eat, and, after his insulin shots, he would be famished. Yet he still guarded his consumption and tried to share his food with his children. His sight had failed, but he could still see during the day and in well-lit places.

Dressed in her Sunday church clothes to appear polished and sophisticated, Violeta boarded a plane for the first time, bound for Dubai, the buzzing city and bustling metropolitan center of the seven emirates comprising the United Arab Emirates. She read as much as she could about the city during her long trip. As was the case for most Asian workers, her contract locked her into two years abroad, regardless of homesickness or an unpleasant situation. However, salaries were good and accommodations were provided for hotel staff. Things were looking promising and exciting. Before the mirror in the plane's toilet, Violeta practiced speaking to staff and receiving royals and celebrities at her beautiful, chic hotel.

An hour before she landed, homesickness struck Violeta, and she wept. The flight attendant noticed that she was crying and chatted with her. The attendant was half-Filipino and half-Italian. She told Violeta what a wonderful place Dubai was, and how she was dating a handsome half-Lebanese, half-Italian graphic designer working in Abu Dhabi. She told her that she would have to be dragged back to the Philippines. In fact, there were so many Filipinos in Dubai that she never had a chance to miss home. They cooked together, celebrated birthdays together, and saw the sights together. But to Violeta it was not home she was thinking of. It was the responsibility of providing for her siblings and parents, and paying off the loan sharks who could be villainous if she was late in paying, charging even more ridiculous rates.

At the Dubai airport, the company chauffeur, a middle-aged, big-bellied and stern-looking Indian with a thick moustache and dark clothes, met Violeta and the other new employees on the same flight. She handed him her suitcase and got into a minivan with several other Filipinas. Everyone was polite, but curt. They secretly began measuring themselves up against their colleagues and thinking of which position they would handle—day manager, night manager, lobby receptionist, bartender, maitre d'hôtel, or waiter.

The drive was short, roughly ten minutes, and the women were shepherded into a hall. Mrs Santos, a middle-aged Filipina dressed in a gray tailored suit, the head of human resources for the company, received them. She asked their names and ages, and if the trip was comfortable. From what the girls had understood, each would go to a different hotel. The lucky ones would go to the five-star hotels near downtown, which meant more tourists and higher tips. The uptown area was slower and more relaxed, but the tips and raises were lower. However, it also was more stable with less chance of being sacked. Mrs Santos casually walked around and inspected the girls, asking them a question at most, and then whispering to her gay, fidgety assistant, who would grunt or whine a response.

Some of the girls were sent to one accommodation, and the rest, including Violeta, went to another. The driver took a highway that led to the outskirts of the city and then into the desert. The shining skyscrapers of Dubai shrank in the distance. After half an hour, all they could see was the great Burj Khalifa towering alone on the horizon.

To Violeta, the landscape looked like something out of a movie—no trees, no bushes, and no greenery of any kind. She squinted against the glare of the sun-drenched sand. She saw two dark shapes moving in the distance: a mother camel trailed by her baby. Violeta wondered how they managed to survive in such a barren land. She missed the greenery of her village and the jungles around it, where it would rain for days and the wet earth would fill the air with the scent of fresh life. Her youngest sister would always make her a hot cup of tea as soon as she was home. She would miss it sorely.

After another hour, the van pulled up to a concrete building. It looked like a lonely labor camp in the middle of the desert. Violeta could not stop comparing it in her mind to Alcatraz prison, which she had seen in the movies. The building was a plain white-washed building of four floors with railed windows. There were air-conditioning boxes in every other window on the lower floor and fewer on the higher floors.

The girls were led one by one to their rooms. Violeta had a small room with no windows, only a wall fan and a lazy rotating fan above her bed. She had a ceiling fan in the Philippines that she always found uncomfortable to sleep under after a shower or walking home in the rain, as she would end up with a cold.

She unpacked her things and looked around the room. The lack of windows and the single bulb hanging from the ceiling seemed prison-like, and she began thinking of the flower-patterned lampshades that she used to stretch over thin wire and sell at the Sunday market in her village. She could easily make one to dress up the room. This was going to be her home for the next two years, and she was determined to make the atmosphere homey and cozy.

There was no kitchen, just a single wooden table with a matching chair. The bed was a low queen-sized bed with white sheets. It seemed large for her, but she reveled in the one touch of luxury. A single mirror hung above a white washbasin. On the opposite wall hung a painting of a forest and lake with birds on the horizon. The room was clean and neat, and Violeta thought about where she could put a flowerpot. She could not help feeling like she was in a forced dormitory, a strict Catholic boarding school, or a penitentiary.

When evening came, Mrs Santos summoned everyone on Violeta's floor into the hallway. The girls stood in front of the doors to their rooms like prisoners in front of their cells or nervous soldiers meeting their general for the first time. Mrs Santos gave each young woman a Panadol and a sip of water from a small paper cup. "This will help you sleep better," she said.

Violeta could not help but feel like she was back in Catholic girls school and Mrs Santos was the priest, giving the sacramental wafer. Mrs Santos said she was being supportive of her fellow *kabayans* because they needed to be bright-eyed for the next day. The young women were all nervous, curious, and guarded as they took the pill before going to bed. Violeta slept soundly, for which she was grateful because she had not stopped thinking of her family and her hopes of changing everything for the best.

She woke the next day feeling dizzy and lazy. She went to the bathroom but had to wait twenty minutes for a shower. The conversation among the women was friendlier than the day before. It was an international group made up of young women from the Philippines, India, Pakistan, Indonesia, Armenia, Romania, Moldova, Ukraine, Morocco, and Egypt. Apparently none of them measured up for working in the posh hotels, as they had been sent to this hostel until further notice. All seemed pretty and full of promise. A few were weepy and others prayed that they could climb up the ladder.

Violeta's tears ran like a stream in the hot shower. She felt like she had poured her last asset down the drain.

She was determined to speak to Mrs Santos, *kabayan* to *kabayan*. Surely Mrs Santos could find her a better position. Lucas had said his colleague's girlfriend and friends were all working in Abu Dhabi and Sharjah as cooks, maids, tailors, receptionists, manicurists, and teachers' assistants. Could they help? She could not go back to the Philippines now. She could work as a maid for $200 a month for two years and be fine, since the family would provide meals and accommodations.

Claustrophobia began to set in. Violeta disliked how she and her colleagues were herded like cattle into the halls. She could not shake off the jet lag. That morning Mrs Santos said that due to their appearance, they would not work in a hotel. Ever. Some of the women started weeping and blowing their noses, making a dull murmur in the background. Violeta stood up and asked what kind of work they were supposed to do. She pointed out that she had personally pawned her last asset to be able to work; she did not mention that she was the sole breadwinner and needed some job—any job—to support her dependent family. She stood there, looking at Mrs Santos, demanding an answer politely but firmly, hoping she would not notice her trembling fingers.

That was when the gates of hell opened.

Mrs Santos said that the women would receive a bed and meals plus a salary of $136 a month to entertain customers.

"My dear, the most I can do for you is to introduce you to your customers, and you will be taken care of." She paused to see if her meaning was clear. "This means you will have to sleep with your customers," Mrs Santos added quietly and ever so coolly, as if she were asking if Violeta would like one cube of sugar for her tea, or two.

Silence swept through the room, then a murmur, and then as things were explained voices were raised and tones were sharper. The twenty young women began to shout at Mrs Santos. The noise was louder than anyone could comprehend. Mrs Santos told the newcomers that the entire four-story building was full of women prostituting themselves. She said it casually and lightly as if it were common practice. They all had signed contracts, and they would be compensated. She added that she was fair and kind. She said that after the two-year contract the girls could leave with their compensation and a bonus. She smiled as she said it.

Violeta went to her room to pack and leave. She would walk to the airport and head back home. Part-time jobs were available, or the family could sell part of the land. Her thoughts were racing and she was crying when quietly and quickly a strong figure came up from behind and put a handkerchief soaked in something over her mouth. Violeta was unconscious by the second breath she took.

When she awoke, her wrists and ankles had been tied to the bed. She was too drugged to yell for help, and she was still under the notion that she was back in her province. She felt that there was someone in the room, but she could not make out who it was. She was so sleepy that the fan did not even bother her.

She woke up at night with the scent of a musky men's cologne in the air, or was it on the sheets? Mrs Santos walked in and began speaking indistinctly about how she would get used to it. She told Violeta she had serviced three men already, but Violeta was too drugged to fully understand. Her tied hands itched. She sat up, but the drugs affected her balance, and she lay down once again. There was a dull pain in her private parts. Her body felt mangled.

Mrs Santos stroked Violeta's hair and dried her face with a handkerchief. Violeta was too drugged to even wipe away her tears. Food was brought in and Violeta was left alone. She had been doped and raped, and she could not do anything about it. She did not even see their faces, these men who had taken her so intimately. She did not even know their names.

A single pill would be left next to a bottle of water on the table for her to take in case she was to get pregnant. She felt like an animal in a cave. Sometimes she would fight, but that would mean being injected with more drugs, and then she would service more men and be left feeling sore and sometimes bruised by the sadistic few. She fought during the first few weeks, but eventually began taking the pills to ease the pain, to protect against pregnancy, and to sleep. The women were turned into drugged bodies to be able to handle the emotional pressure of the situation.

This was going to be her life for the next two years. She serviced as many as fifteen customers a day of different classes, nationalities, and ages. She begged the Filipino men to notify the embassy, but they did not help and sometimes never came back to her. Some men told her to wear a cotton mask to prevent the spread of germs. Some would beat her if she refused, so she became obedient and never fought back.

As the days passed, there was no need to be tied down. Apathy descended upon the girls, who serviced a minimum of five men a day. The women were not allowed out, so others wired money to their families. The women were told that after two years they had the option of either going back to their homes or continuing their job. The flock of sheep that they were, the women sought refuge in each other's pain and stories. Some eventually gave in, but when they did, they were never the same again. They stopped complaining and even stopped talking. They became robots that wanted nothing more than for the day to end. Some attempted suicide. A few managed to kill themselves. The rest were broken into the trade by six months.

The customers were working class, single and married men. They knew the women were forced into prostitution and kept captive, and sometimes they would chat if they were sober. If they were drunk, they could get aggressive. Men were not allowed to bring sharp objects to the bedrooms. Sometimes the women would miss a fellow prisoner and would hear through whispers that she had been killed; some had been strangled, others left to bleed to death. Mrs Santos tried to keep everyone awake so they could scream if the customer became violent.

Human trafficking is illegal everywhere, but people everywhere still do it. Some are forced into it. Others are addicted to heroin, cocaine, and other hard drugs and servicing clients was the only way to get a continued supply from the drug sellers. Sometimes female members of a household were pawned or held responsible for a drunken father or gambling husband. Violeta met European women who had been imprisoned in a hostel in Serbia and then flown to the UAE. Many were happy about the change, since they would one day earn their freedom, while European prisoners never got out.

Mrs Santos constantly told Violeta and the other girls that she was their partner, that she only gave them pills, which was a light drug. She said that in the city men drove around, luring Filipina, Ethiopian and Indonesian maids who had gone grocery shopping into running away and working "part time" where they would have independence, more pay and travel to Europe. The maids would join and then be trapped in the man's apartment and forced to service clients there. If the man was desperate—a gambler or a drunk—he would lower the price, letting in as many clients as possible for as little as possible, because he simply did not care. All he cared about was collecting money for his habit at the end of the day. These were the worst situations for a woman to be in—far worse than where they were.

Violeta had read about Stockholm Syndrome and could see it developing all around her. Some of the girls grew attached to Mrs Santos for the small kindnesses she showed and for her honesty, forgetting she was their captor. Violeta found herself feeling grateful that she was not piercing her veins with the narcotics.

One morning a drug-addicted European prisoner sliced her wrists in the shower and bled to death. When Violeta walked into the shower, the woman's eyes were open, the shower was running, and her long, orange hair reached to her waist, covering her breasts. With her legs folded to one side, she looked like the Little Mermaid, and shared the same ending.

Violeta cried for the woman and for herself. The woman's heart had taken more than her body could handle. Violeta knew the woman and knew she had lost count of how many years she had been in the trade and how many abortions she had had. The woman suffered from partial amnesia of certain episodes of her life. She forgot the faces of her children, and she would cry and walk around with a pillow, thinking it was her baby. In Europe, the woman had not been taken care of by her madam, Mrs Santos said, using the episode to remind her prisoners of how much better off they were.

The police discovered the brothel one night and barged into the rooms. The women screamed, thinking they were in trouble, but the police were not there to take them to jail. They were there to set them free. Only the women's keepers were arrested. Violeta saw Mrs Santos in handcuffs being escorted by a police officer. Her head was bowed, in prayer or in shame, as she was led to the police van.

Violeta was sent to live in the Dubai Charity Home, a shelter for abused women. She stayed there for two years, recuperating physically and emotionally. She took up music while in recovery and found solace in it, playing the piano with such passion that it became an adventure, a tragedy, and a murderous romance all in one. Through music, the spell of abuse was broken.

Violeta left the shelter, but was so moved by the experience that she decided to work in one as a way of helping others who had been put in similar circumstances. She now teaches music therapy to victims of human trafficking at a shelter in Dubai, earning enough money to put her siblings through college.

Sleeping with the Nanny

I WAS SEATED NEXT TO my husband, Eissa, when the brain surgeon at Hamad General Hospital in Doha, Qatar, informed us that my partner of seventeen years had brain cancer. Had it been another form of cancer I might have reacted more collectedly, as recovery rates for many forms of cancer are well above fifty percent. But brain cancer is different. Its recovery rates remain low, and its treatment is difficult and painful. My father had died of another deadly form of cancer, lung cancer, and the nightmare of his agony flashed before me. Cancer was taking everyone I loved from me. When were they going to invent a cure for this Black Death?

I was engulfed in fear, for here was the man I loved, at the age of thirty-nine, fighting for his life. And so began the long, emotionally exhausting journey of treatments, tests, and scans to check whether the cancer was shrinking or growing. This put a strain on all of us: my husband, me, our children, and our nanny, Veronica, who had cared for my husband since he was a child and now was helping us to raise our five children. It seemed like every ounce of energy was being drained out of our bodies. All

I wanted was for my husband and our lives to return to normal.

Throughout the travels to Germany and the UK to see cancer specialists, the hospital stays, tests, treatments, and loss of hair, Veronica was with him. As I watched how close they were, it seemed heartwarming, but slowly it turned into something else, something unseemly and almost incestuous. Ashamed of my suspicions, I punished myself for thinking the way I did. I was being selfish and jealous at a time when maturity was required. However, the situation did not make handling Eissa's illness any easier.

The cancer treatment was as cruel as it was long, and my husband began to wilt away. The whole family was affected; I had to be the rock for them, and I was. Normally I loved to watch the leaves change color in the fall, but the year of Eissa's hospitalization in London, the fading of the trees from vibrant green to dry autumnal colors reminded me of how my husband was losing his hair, strength, and weight. My four sons all came home one day with shaved heads, saying it was in support of their father so he would not feel that he was the only one that had no hair on his head.

Each day, my husband ate less of his bland food. Fear gripped me like a child clutching at her parting mother. Yet through all of this I did not falter. I maintained my nerves and only cried in secret. My four boys and young daughter clung to whatever we had of Eissa's pictures and memories. We exhausted every occasion with picture taking because we were so afraid that he would not make it that we wanted every living moment together to be recorded. An entire wall of the apartment we had rented in London was covered with framed pictures, pinned-up letters, cards, souvenirs, and keepsakes.

As the season's colors faded, the color drained from Eissa's face and hair as well. He seemed frailer with every leaf that fell. I tried to revive him and cheer him up on a daily basis. It went without saying that with an ailing husband, I was expected to turn into iron woman physically and emotionally. Over and over I would carry him to the bathroom and bathe him. I dried him with more attention and care than I did my own children because I felt I was caring for something I was losing. My children's lives were growing brighter, more bustling, and more vivacious every day. The comparison popped into my mind every time I cleaned my husband and dressed him. Gratefully, I joined a support group in the hospital for relatives of cancer patients. We would talk, relate, and build each other up for another day. This familiarity with similar calamities helped me to calm down and withstand the hardships of being in a foreign country, alone, with my husband's condition deteriorating every day.

As winter approached, my husband's health suddenly and unexpectedly improved. His ashen lips regained the red blush of youth and his voice, which had grown faint and cracked during the treatment, recovered its masculine depth and resonance. He spoke more often and poked fun at his children, joking about how they had to be nice to him because he was the sick one. The mood in the hospital room lightened for a change.

Winter was thawing into a welcome spring; the flowers sent by friends were as soul-lifting as they were scented. The whole room smelled of flowers, lending some well-deserved happiness and gaiety to the once-stagnant, gloomy air. Visiting hours were granted, and each day we would have a few pleasant visitors who would drop by with food that even Eissa could eat and enjoy with us. The first time he ate without vomiting I cried in relief. It had been a hard journey, and I was so proud of his recovery, however difficult and painful it had been.

As spring approached, Eissa came home to our London apartment. We found ourselves going less and less often to the hospital for checkups. The children and I were at peace once again; their father was getting better. Even his eyebrows, lashes, and hair were growing back, thicker and more lustrous. He was a man with a sense of humor and would always say, "Don't forget to buy me hair spray, because I need to pick up on my modeling career after this vacation."

I loved his personality. He was a breath of fresh air, and he helped me to get over this ordeal even more than I helped him. He was the love of my life. He was grateful to all of us, and we were so fortunate to be able to have a longer time with such a wonderful figure. In all this time he was polite, apologetic, and supportive to every person of the family. He would repeatedly say he was sorry for the trouble he caused when we would have to clean up after him or aid him in movement.

At last, our lives had become normal again. The bliss was short-lived, however. The disease did not return, but my suspicions about Veronica did. One day, I went to the gym only to find that I had forgotten my workout shirt and shoes. I got back in my car and returned home. Veronica was home with my husband as usual, but when I entered I noticed that the two of them were acting guarded and nervous. I was planning to return to the gym, but when I saw their behavior I changed my mind. Veronica in particular was acting skittish. When she broke a dish in the kitchen, my thoughts raced.

I went into the bedroom and found my husband in the shower—a technique he employed whenever he wanted to escape a conversation or confrontation. I saw his mobile phone, and my instinct told me to pry into it. Mobiles are the secrets to a man's soul, or so it seems nowadays.

The password was our anniversary. He used to say it was the real day he was born. I was bothered when I read a few messages from Veronica, asking him when he was going to join her.

Going on with the messages, I found a few with no text, only images of her in the shower, blowing kisses and winking at him. The images were enough. This fifty-five-year-old Filipina maid was his lover. The kids were coming back soon, so I called to my husband to come out of the shower.

"What are you yelling about?" he asked, visibly annoyed at my raised voice.

"I'll show you what I'm yelling about," I said, shoving the image of Veronica in his face.

"Where did you get that?" he shouted.

"It's your phone, sweetheart," I said mockingly. "Don't you remember? Your password is our anniversary, 'the day you were truly born'?"

He tried to grab the phone from my hand, but I pulled it away and threw it as hard as I could against the wall.

"Don't worry about your pictures of Veronica," I said. "I'm sure there are more just like them on 'hot grandmas dot com.'"

I burst out crying and ran down the hall to Veronica's room. My husband and I had been arguing in Arabic, so I doubted if she understood what was happening.

"I know what you have been doing with my husband," I yelled in English. "How could you?"

She just stood there, looking at me as tears ran down my face. "I'm sorry, Mam," she said at last. "But . . ."

"But what?" I screamed.

"I was his first love."

I turned to my husband, who was standing outside the doorway like a child.

"This woman is married with children. And grandchildren!" I screamed. "She is old enough to be your mother. This cannot be real!"

The improbability of this union in terms of age, race, religion, and status seemed grotesque and incestuous. It was as crazy as crazy gets. I glared at my husband.

"Send her back to the Philippines," I said through my teeth. He glanced over my shoulder at Veronica and then looked down.

"Cancel her visa and send her back!" I shouted.

Staring at the floor, my husband shook his head. "I can't do that," he said.

"You can and you will. Today."

"I won't do it," he said at last. "I love her."

"Let me make this simple for you," I said. "It's either me, the mother of your children, or her. One of us has to go!"

I knew he could not refuse when I put it that way. The ultimate ultimatum. He was a good father and I knew he loved me. I could not see what he saw in her. She was old, short, apple-bodied, and had no attractive features. Veronica was speaking quickly, but my mind was swimming and my world was shaking.

He shrugged. "I'm sorry," he said.

My universe crumbled. Everything I knew, or thought I knew, came flying apart like an exploding star. I was shattered into pieces; a woman of lesser spirit would have been crushed completely, but not me.

I composed myself, gathered up the children, and left. I put up a strong front; I had to, for the sake of my kids—I did not want them to know. The summer had just started and school was off for now. I would go back home and retreat into my cave, lick my wounds, and figure out what had happened.

I booked a flight home to Qatar from Gatwick for the children and myself. On the plane trip, I plotted how to bring my husband back to my arms, no matter what. My children needed their father, and I needed my life partner. Veronica would have to go back to her twisted life, husband, children, and grandchildren.

After arriving in Doha, I spoke to my mother-in-law. She was disappointed in her son, even outraged, but she did not seem shocked.

"It's unbelievable, isn't it?" I said.

My mother-in-law looked at her hands, folded in her lap.

"What is it?" I asked.

She looked up at me and wiped a tear from her eye. "No, it's not unbelievable," she said quietly. "It is all too believable. We've heard many similar stories, but no one chooses the maid over the wife. Please calm yourself down, it will be all right. No one leaves the wife. What about his children? He loves you and his children. You have to be strong."

My mother-in-law seemed convinced that he was going to come back. She called it a "phase," one that he had not outgrown. She described how Veronica was always with him when he traveled, studying abroad or taking summer vacations. The reason was revealed and the truth was made clear, and it was repulsive.

"What do you mean?" I asked. "Veronica is fifty-five years old, her charms have faded, and she is our employee. Look at me and tell me what is believable about it?"

"Before he married you, his father and I learned that Veronica had been his lover since he was twelve years old," she said, wiping away another tear. "She went to Eissa's room one night, probably to say goodnight, and noticed that Eissa, the boy, her boy, had become a man. She slept with my little boy, and latched on to him. I thought it was just a phase . . ." Her voice trailed off. The seed had been planted deep and had grown into a bad habit.

My mother-in-law and I sat analyzing the puzzle and putting it together, piece by piece. We discussed all the clues from throughout the years; how we were so naïve and how we chose to turn a blind eye to the obvious. After all Veronica was a woman, far away from her husband, and Eissa was available. He trusted her, and she, him. She molded him to her likes, and he molded her to his.

"She told us that he had a bedwetting problem and that in the Philippines an adult would sleep in the same room with the child to make them feel safe or wake them at night to take them to the bathroom. The plan served her well. We never noticed anything out of the ordinary or thought ill of her. On the contrary, we were grateful for the kind and thoughtful nanny we had. We did not realize that she mothered him during the day and was his lover at night.

"We learned of the affair about the time you became engaged. We sat both of them down and told them it had to stop. We told Veronica that we would cancel her work visa and send her back to the Philippines if she so much as gave our boy a look. They both agreed to end the affair, and she stopped going to his room at night. Everything seemed back to normal. She had been a great support when our children were young, almost a member of our family, so I thought she could be of great use to you as well. With a beautiful bride like you, I was sure he wouldn't even notice her, let alone do anything like this."

I was sure that once my husband and Veronica were alone, he would see her for what she was. The appeal of the forbidden fruit would be gone. In its place would be the fig that turns to ash in the mouth. But I was wrong. The spell she had over him was not broken. I was grateful that my mother-in-law was on my side, but I was deeply distressed that such a thing could happen with the people we allow into our lives, those we trust to care for our children.

Then, as if the forces of heaven had conspired to support me, I found out that my husband's mistress had to leave for her home country. Her mother had died and she wanted to attend the burial. Our old driver sent me a message that he had just dropped Veronica off at the airport; she had left for Manila. This was my chance to put them apart and plan my return. I truly believed that he was with her because she was blackmailing him emotionally. I made some phone calls to cancel her visa, making sure she would never be able to return. I had her banned from the country. I felt like a victorious warrior who had vanquished her foe. In my heart of hearts, I had hoped that this would finally lead my husband back to my arms.

Sadly, Eissa was still beguiled by his mistress and did everything he could to bring her back. He refused to see us, any of us, even his mother. Even his daughter's calls and voice messages did not move a hair on his body. His father had passed away long ago, so I had no person of authority left to create a presence with him, make demands upon him, or control him. His mother would cry and beg him to end this embarrassing affair and come to his senses. He respected her, but would not bend. I tried to contact him, to see him, believing he would surely miss me and our family. The children missed their father. His absence had left a gaping hole in the family, one that we wore on our faces. People would inquire after him and we would stare back blankly and answer curtly that all was well.

Giving Veronica a new identity was the only way for her to return, so Eissa paid for a new passport to be made for her in the Philippines. The forgery completed, Veronica made a triumphant return to Qatar, living in our house with my husband while I lived in my parents' house with our kids. I could not tell them the truth for fear of shame and being on everyone's gossip grapevine for as long as my children and I would live. I languished in sorrow, with almost no hope of ever having my husband back.

Two years later, Veronica returned to the Philippines to see her family on her biannual leave. I again tried to have her banned. This time when she returned, the new security equipment scanned her eyes and her false identity was exposed. The immigration officers confiscated her forged passport and sent her home on the next plane. She was added to the registry of banned travelers and would be denied entry when she returned. This included the rest of the Gulf states as well. She was out of my hair at last. The spell would soon be broken, and I would finally win.

My husband and I had been separated a few years by the time I succeeded in preventing Veronica's return. Once she was gone, Eissa tried to make things right with me almost immediately. He asked me to come back to our house, and I agreed for the children's sake and because I still loved him.

Still, I was broken by what had happened. I tried to convince myself that it was not his fault and to place the blame on everyone except him. His mother did not look after him closely enough, the maid was mad and controlling, and I was weak because I played the mother, wife and secretary role all in one. Veronica understood him better than I did, better than his own mother did, and probably better than he did, himself. She came from a poor background and was grateful for whatever scraps she would get of his time, and he would be calm with her and ever so content, whereas I always demanded quantity and quality time from him.

Yet having said and thought that, I was still hurt. I felt uprooted, betrayed, and taken for granted. My primary reason for coming back to him was the children, but it also was because he was all that I knew a man to be; I possessed too much love for him to simply leave. I needed him back for more reasons than reason could comprehend. With a broken heart, I returned to my traitor.

He apologized repeatedly, saying it was complicated and he did not know what to do. He wanted both her and me, but I was the one creating a ruckus. He blamed me for leaving, and I blamed Veronica. But Veronica was gone. It was the end of that episode. Defeating Veronica had been harder than defeating cancer in my book and measure.

The hand that rocks the cradle rules the world, one saying goes. Veronica the nanny had ruled my husband's world. The bond that had formed between them during Eissa's youth became so strong over the years that even the sanctity of our marriage could not break it. I still dream of her every now and then. She is in her early sixties now and, thanks to my husband, is quite well off in her province with her family well-settled and taken care of.

Communication finally ceased between them after Shereena, our youngest child, fell sick and stopped speaking. We eventually took her to a therapist and after testing and reviewing her condition the doctor said that her silence was due to trauma induced by emotional instability and pent-up anger. I broke down that night and blamed Eissa for hurting her. He did not understand and thought that I was exaggerating. I told him that Shereena was emotionally scarred because he had abandoned her for years for his nanny.

The girl who was the sunniest and brightest of her classmates and chattiest of her siblings had retreated into a cave of rejection. She was ten years old and simply stopped caring for anything in the world. She developed anorexia and stopped eating. Her wrists had thin silver lines of small slits, cuts that she inflicted upon herself. Self-harm is one of the most unhealthy ways of dealing with pain, intense anger, and frustration. It brought Shereena a temporary sense of calm and a release of tension but would be followed by a vicious cycle of guilt, shame and a resurfacing of emotional pain. And scars that wouldn't fade. My only daughter, Shereena, was diagnosed with depression at ten years old. She seldom spoke and had no friends. It had taken a boulder to hit us for my husband to wake up from his late adolescence.

"What have I done?" he said as he sat one day, looking at pictures of Shereena's file from Hamad Hospital. "Do you know that when I spoke to her about why she was harming herself, she cried and begged me not to leave her again?"

"She was the most affected by you leaving, you know," I said. "She stopped letting me read her stories because I would read them in your bed, where you would do the funny voices. I think it reminded her of you too much. You don't know how much your absence has hurt the kids. Your boys clean their own rooms and won't even see the maids now."

I was honest, and did not feel the need to sugarcoat the fact that we were all reaping what he had sown.

"They are all still very hurt, both for me and for their own identity," I said. "You were their idol, their father, and their rock. They feel cheated and are so afraid for me because of your immaturity."

A tear ran down my cheek, all the way to my neck, and I did not bother to wipe it. How can one person ruin and burn a whole family with so many people involved? We, who had once decorated our walls in pride and love, had instead decorated our funeral pyre, creating a constant reminder of a love we once had for someone who clearly did not love us back enough to care.

Eissa severed all relations with Veronica, no longer calling her or wiring her money. Eventually, Shereena built herself up and stopped self-harming, but she was never as vivacious as she once had been. She wants to enter the healing practice of either psychiatry or medicine when she is older. Her brothers are delaying marriage. As for me, my marriage is back on track. Eissa never speaks of the past, nor do the children bring it up. He constantly tells them that they are his pride, they are his rock, and they are the father because they are wiser than their years.

I prayed for him to come back, and I am grateful to have my life back to normal. We normally think of men warping the lives of young women by introducing them to sex at an early age, but my Eissa was living proof that a woman can do the same thing by sexualizing a boy when he is not mature enough to handle the contact.

Crazy for You

MY HUSBAND WALEED WAS twenty-two when we married. He had graduated with a degree in business administration from a leading university in Boston. I, Rasha, was eighteen and fresh out of high school. We bought an apartment in Jeddah with a joint account to start our married life together. I became pregnant for the first time while at university studying and working, but with Waleed's love and support was able to finish the semester. I gave birth to twin daughters during the summer break. My husband hired a nanny, allowing me to go back to school in the fall. I became pregnant again my senior year but with the help of my husband and the nanny was able to graduate with my own degree in business. Shortly after finishing university, I had our third child—a boy.

As my husband was working his way up in his business, I wanted to help pay the mortgage on our beautiful new four-bedroom villa so I took a part-time job in the accounting department of a prestigious girls' university. I worked hard on my family and home, hiring and training a maid to keep the house exactly as I wanted it and coaching the nanny to help the children with development games. I did everything I could to support my husband financially and emotionally, keeping a tight budget, avoiding frivolous expenditures, and saving as much as possible.

My husband was attentive to his family's needs while still making time to visit elderly members of the family and check on the academic and professional development of his siblings. He followed through with everyone: his friends and even the maid's daughter who was the first of her family to finish school thanks to his support. I would come up with ideas to efficiently help his friends when they would need money and guidance. Everyone would be invited to donate what they had, where and when they could, and every little bit helped. He was remembered for it and was a hero in everyone's eyes. They say that behind every successful man is a strong woman, and he knew it. We were a team, and a winning one at that, an example of happy and fruitful cooperation. We failed in some of our investments and succeeded in others but we learned to depend on each other as each of us was the other's better half.

Sometimes I missed our time alone together and felt that he was spending too much time investing in other people and living for the future. He always promised that he would make it up to me, and I saw in his success our ultimate satisfaction and victory. I envisioned our dreams for the future: travel, and tweaking our looks with minor plastic surgery, polishing our skills and boosting our confidence with self-help and development seminars. Paris in autumn with fresh baguettes and cheese, walking along the Seine after placing a lock with my name and my husband's on it. I wanted to go on a pilgrimage of faith to Mecca where I would pray shoulder to shoulder with him and tell God how grateful I was for my health, wealth, beautiful children, and the opportunity to live life like we chose to. Hawaiian sun had always sounded like the dream honeymoon to start with after we actually had time and money.

Often, we would discuss how things would be easier once we were debt-free. Money was a continuous struggle, but we were organized, careful adults with measured and well thought-out plans. My husband dreamed of investing in his own business franchise and expanding it throughout the region. From his years studying abroad, Waleed had developed an interest in restaurant franchising. He saw how Gulf residents were flocking to Western restaurants and dreamed of building a chain of his own. The idea of introducing new cuisine to his homeland excited him. A humanitarian, he looked forward to employing migrant workers from Asia and Africa who were eager to better themselves and support their families back home. He admired American-style team building and had excelled during his internships in the United States. I saw the world through his eyes, and it was a vision I was proud to share. I learned to improve my English so I would be able to play a more active role in his world. I loved Meryl Streep, Audrey Hepburn, and Angelina Jolie. They were strong women, and I respected how they persisted, worked, and played the roles of mother and wife so elegantly.

Our joint loan on Waleed's franchise had begun to reap returns. The food industry is never a bad idea, and people always need to eat, even during an economic crisis. Our children grew up in and around the restaurants, learning the ins and outs of the business. Through his restaurants, Waleed expanded his circle of friends and associates and we were able to find outstanding matches for our daughters. The profits from the business also enabled us to send our son to the finest university in Australia.

Deena and Leena, my dentist daughters, had beautiful weddings a few months apart. Deena held hers at the beach which was uncommon, but she wanted a simple ceremony and close friends. Leena had a big wedding in a hotel with 700 guests. She insisted on a singer, which cost a fortune that was shared between us and the groom. The favors, cards, and centerpieces were exceptionally beautiful, with Victorian-themed details of velvet, lace, and rococo grandeur that demanded gilt, glitter, shine, and luxury. My son, Talal, had a dinner reception and married our neighbor's daughter, Yasmeen. He had always loved her, and her family was friendly, kind, and well-reputed. We were all delighted with the union.

As our financial burdens ebbed, our life began to get easier, and as we sat down to dinner one day I suggested to Waleed that maybe this summer would be a good time for us to finally take the round-the-world trip he was always promising. We had had children when we were young, when it felt like the natural and expected thing to do.

Now maturity called upon us to explore both new lands and ourselves. My husband thought the trip around the world was a thrilling idea. We talked about places we had never been but often thought about—South America, the Pacific Islands, much of Asia. As I was daydreaming about getting away from it all, my husband said he wanted to discuss something with me as well. I did not travel much, but loved the way his face would light up as he would share his traveling tales. I acquired his travel addiction and looked forward to it with him.

"Of course," I said, excited to hear what he had to say.

"I want you to have an open mind," he said.

"I don't know what that means," I said. "I always have an open mind."

"I don't want you to say no without thinking about it," he said. "It's important to me."

"If it's important to you, I'm sure it will be important to me."

He smiled. "I want to take a second wife," he said.

My heart stopped. He knocked the breath out of my chest, and I sat there staring. I wanted him to finish his sentence and say otherwise. I looked at him to see if he was kidding. "Sweetheart, you can barely keep up with the one you have," I joked. "What are you going to do with a second one?"

"I'm serious," he said.

"If you want another flavor, take a trip," I said. "Satisfy your craving and come back."

"It's not that," he said. "I have fallen in love."

"It *is* that," I said, "and you are just telling yourself it's not so you do not feel guilty."

"That's not true."

"Who is it?" I asked. "Please tell me it's not someone I know." I felt a knot forming in my stomach, threatening to reach my throat.

"It's not. She's a young entrepreneur who wants to launch a restaurant chain. She came to me for advice, and I have spent the last few months showing her my restaurants and scouting out possible locations for hers."

"Have you slept with her?" I asked, trying to keep my voice steady in spite of the shock and pain that I felt coursing through my body.

"No. You know me. I would never do that."

"I thought I knew you, but now I'm not sure." The man sitting across from me, my husband, suddenly seemed like a stranger, someone I could no longer fathom.

"Listen. Please do not think of this as any kind of criticism or dissatisfaction with you. You know I love, admire, and depend on you. But think about how much we enjoyed launching our business together. That is the stage that she is at. I want to recapture it. I want to relive it."

"This is not about business."

"Partly it is—sharing the adventure. I admire her. I've learned a lot from her. And I've fallen in love with her. Believe me, I did not intend to."

"It just happened," I said, anticipating the cliché. I felt waves of nausea churning my stomach.

"Yes! It just happened."

"Is she beautiful?"

"Not as beautiful as you are."

"That's one thing I have always liked about you, Waleed: You are a terrible liar. I can always tell when you are not telling the truth. How old is she? Or should I say, how young is she?"

"Thirty-five."

"So less than twenty years younger than you are. Congratulations on not robbing the cradle. What nationality is she?"

"Lebanese," he said, his voice barely audible in shame.

"Of course she is," I said. "Well, forget about me supporting you on your voyage of discovery. And forget about ours, too. I will go by myself."

I hid it well, but my mind was reeling and deep inside I was writhing with countless emotions. I could not understand where I had come up short and what had justified his decision. For so many years he never so much as looked at another woman, in part because I had stood by his side, supporting him in every way to build his business.

Determined to stop him, I inquired in the local Fatwa Office about whether he could do this.

"Have you borne him children?" asked the interviewer.

"Yes. Three—two girls and a boy," I said, emphasizing the boy.

"And did you contribute anything financially to the marriage?"

"I did. I worked part time when I graduated university and I managed the finances to build up the capital he needed to launch his business."

"Were you a loving wife throughout the marriage?"

"Yes. Very," I said. "And he was a loving husband. We were happy. Very happy."

"Of course he has the right to a second marriage," said the official, "unless the second marriage ruins, hurts or breaks the first."

"That is why I am here," I said. "It is destroying my husband's integrity in my eyes and crushing what little respect I have for myself. I will not make it."

"That is not what I meant," said the interviewer. "I mean, will this marriage impede your husband's ability to provide for your children?"

"Our daughters are married, and our son is on his own now," I admitted.

"What about you? Will it impact your level of support? Will you be able to continue living as you are accustomed?"

"Living as I am accustomed?" I repeated. "I am not accustomed to sharing my husband with another woman. Who does this nowadays? Cavemen? My husband is an educated man. He lived in America for years. Apparently it did nothing to modernize his thinking."

"Please, madame. I mean financially. Will you be affected?"

"Not financially, no. Only in every other way."

"I will submit your application, but I cannot be encouraging," said the interviewer.

I lost every battle, but I was determined to win the war. Citing a common practice in Saudi Arabia and Kuwait when housing two wives, I told Waleed that I would agree to his second marriage if he signed over the first floor of the house to me. Eager to avoid conflict, he readily agreed.

He began preparing for his wedding and I began planning my revenge. The day he married his precious protégée, I filed for divorce. Since he was getting married, the court granted the divorce instantly. By the time he was on his honeymoon, I was enjoying my sweet, cold revenge. He had originally planned to take her to Hawaii, on our trip. I demanded my compensation instantly, and that cut his finances short, so he was forced to divert from Hawaii to Malaysia, which was more affordable and yet seemed similar in terms of islands, sun, and sand. I had a scrapbook of the travel spots we were going to visit in Hawaii. She would never see Pearl Harbor or Sunset Beach, Oahu's hidden beaches or the Waimea Valley where we were planning on going on the volcano tour. I had ruined it all for them.

From the day my husband brought up the topic of getting a new wife, I had been working on my looks and saving money. Without my husband knowing it, he had paid for my breast lift, a lip enhancement, eyelid reduction, and the launch of my cosmetics business. Waleed thought I could not compete with his thirty-something fiance, but by the time they got married she was the one who could not compete with me.

Friends and acquaintances noticed my new look and I began to receive admiring glances I had not seen for quite a while. My attorney's law partner, Nawaf, was one of those who noticed my makeover. He sympathized with the pain I was going through with my husband's choice of a new wife and was friendly and welcoming whenever I came to the office. I started visiting the office more and more as we both came to enjoy one another's company and conversations. He admired my strength and work ethic, especially how I had handled the trials and tribulations of recent months with a level head and steady determination. When he knew I had been granted a divorce, he proposed marriage.

A fit, tall, handsome gentleman, he was a widower at just twenty-nine, having lost his young wife in an accident some years earlier. This tragic loss had matured him beyond his years, making us a good match. I did not want to rush into another marriage, so I publicized our engagement but took my time to get to know him better. He proved to be charismatic and gentle and by all counts seemed to be the answer to my prayers.

Nawaf had taken notice of the teary-eyed woman who would frequent the lawyer, and upon inquiring had found out my circumstances. He respected how I rose to face the storm and wanted to live proud and free. He said that he liked my face and wanted to be able to share his life with me. He said he wanted to be happy, and my happiness made him feel whole.

When Waleed found out that I was engaged, he became furious. My children were frightened for me, worried that their father would hurt Nawaf or me. All my children were against their father's mid-life crisis choice of taking a second wife out of the blue. The children approved of Nawaf. They did not appreciate the pain that my ex-husband had caused and only wanted to see me happy. Of course Waleed would always be their biological father, but he had chosen to leave his family to build a new one and that was something that was unforgivable on an emotional level.

Waleed began stalking me, calling me at all hours of the day and night, texting and emailing me incessantly. I did not care. I really did not. He stopped mattering to me. He had simply ceased to exist and I paid no heed to his childish jealousy and curiosity. I was a free woman now and was spreading my wings, a most engaging experience. My new husband was from a different state and since I did not want to move away from my daughters, he came every weekend to see me.

To keep busy, I launched a social blog, Instagram and Facebook accounts which soon gained many fans, introducing me to many people and helping me to both improve and market my cosmetics business on a more personal level. Business was booming, and I was free to focus on myself and capitalize on things that I had never got around to doing in my first marriage. I became a social butterfly, celebrated as a role model for conquering the business world against all odds and succeeding financially. My ex-husband was against my newfound fame and TV appearances, but it did not matter as he now had no rights over me.

Everyone loved me but at the same time blamed him on so many levels. I passed through the stage of anger and revenge-seeking to feeling sorry for him for the ridicule, pity and disgust people leveled at him for his actions. I simply replied that I had let fate take care of itself.

After I married my sweet, young husband we moved into my house. This was more of a convenient move than a vindictive one as I wanted to remain close to my family, my business, and my new friends. My ex-husband could not believe that I had done this. Here was his ex-wife of twenty-one years living with her attractive, young husband right under his own roof. It was too much for him to bear. My new husband was as handsome as he was suave, the kind of man who would step into a room and make other men nervous, jealous and shaken by his gentle demeanor and firm boldness. Waleed could not stand his new wife looking at Nawaf. Even his name was mysteriously attractive and his smile would win hearts. On occasion, Waleed would check on our children, but their faces would light up for Nawaf while remaining basically unresponsive with Waleed. That hurt him to his very core.

We lived in the same house and I would cross through the ground floor with Nawaf on a daily basis. I felt younger and more attractive every day. In terms of dependence, Nawaf was the opposite of Waleed. Nawaf wanted to help me grow, and we began speaking confidently in English.

My English even surpassed Waleed's. I enjoyed Nawaf teaching me, and we would watch movies together in the living room upstairs. Due to his support, I was at last able to truly pick up the language.

Nawaf was everything that Waleed was not. I went to Mecca with him and we prayed together. I placed a lock with our initials on the Bridge of Love and Remembrance. We went to Hawaii and visited the Kilauea Volcano and enjoyed the sun, love, and nature. I lived my life without pause or interruption, without being someone's secretary, or playing the role of the taken-for-granted wife. Nawaf always wanted me to be happy. He believed in the saying "Happy wife, happy life." I would even speak at self-help seminars, emphasizing how we need to love ourselves more and enjoy our own successes no matter how small they were.

I became a successful face in society while Waleed sank into depression. I did not know because I was too busy embracing my new life. Television shows hosted me and people began to recognize me on the streets and in malls and restaurants. Meanwhile, Waleed began to lose friends, employees, and eventually profits. He tried to speak to me, even work with me, but I had chosen to leave him forever.

He soon began bickering with his new wife and slowly losing his mind. My new husband and I heard them fighting late into the night. On a couple of occasions we heard his young wife screaming, so we called the police. He was admitted to a mental asylum after his second attempt on his wife's life and threatening to take his own.

I am now pregnant with a boy and enjoying my new, full life with a man who truly knows my worth.

From Riches to Rags

M Y FATHER IS A Lebanese dental surgeon in New York. My mother is a half-Lebanese, half-Egyptian accountant who went to the United States in search of a golden future. They were two wandering souls drawn to each other by a shared understanding of the world. Once they found one another, they clicked and were immediately inseparable. After a whirlwind romance that lasted only a few weeks, they were married in a small ceremony on the beach in Malibu, California.

However, once back in New York after the honeymoon the romance died quickly as my mother began to make demands of my father regarding ownership of the house and how he should run his dental office, claiming that she was technically an equal partner in the business. My father was a proud man and had built a successful practice on his own. He resented my mother's interference and the implied criticism that his practice was not doing as well as it could. Furthermore, he did not appreciate the financial control that she forced upon him and felt her persistent inquiries into his property ownership as well as her need to share everything were exaggerated.

Next, her brother, my Uncle Adam, moved in and conveniently forgot to move out. Habitually unemployed,

Uncle Adam made himself a permanent fixture on the sofa in front of the TV, where he always had a bag of sunflower seeds and a cold drink at hand. We had a picture of him and his pot belly, and every time I saw him, he was in front of the TV, casually sitting, guarding his drink and contributing to his ever-growing stomach. He constantly criticized the television shows on offer, gambled on sports, and even had the nerve to ask my father to subscribe to satellite TV so he could watch international football leagues. Uncle Adam never worked and probably got whatever money he had from his sister or his side dealings when he would go out, which was a rare occurrence. My father was reserved, but when his patience finally ran out he told my mother that her brother was no longer welcome in their home. This ignited another battle as my mother took her brother's side, belittling my father for having forgotten his Middle Eastern roots and turning against her family. She argued how family was above all and that especially as strangers in a strange land we must always guard, nourish, and support our own. After all, shouldn't benefits always go to family first? Sharing is caring.

I was born in the eye of the ensuing divorce storm. My mother was on several antidepressants and was constantly angry because she and my father had had a religious wedding instead of a legally binding one. This meant that if they were to get a divorce, she would receive less than she was legally entitled to. Money was always an issue, a life threat and a reason to fight. We had enough, but the insecurities embedded within her were unquenchable. When the divorce was eventually finalized, she could not collect a decent settlement because the marriage was not legally recognized. Furthermore, she was unable to find a job. Because of her unemployment, abuse of antidepressants, and aggressive behavior, the court determined that she was an unfit parent. My father gained full custody of me, and my mother was allowed one supervised visit per week.

I grew up adoring my gentle father, who picked me up from school, sang to me, and read me stories before I went to bed. We went for picnics in spring and built snowmen in Colorado in the winter. Unlike other parents who always were in a hurry to get somewhere, my father would stop whenever I saw a carnival with a Ferris wheel and kiddy rides or a Halloween pumpkin patch with a giant slide. I was happy as a child and wanted for nothing. He had loved my mother and was heartbroken after the divorce, and so he compensated by being overly loving with me.

In contrast to the feelings toward my father, I did not particularly like the "Mother" who would come once a week to lecture me, greeting me with knitted eyebrows, a smirk, and a sarcastic comment. She always had something negative to say about my father and always made comments about how ungrateful I was to have silks, furs, and velvet for clothes. She said that I lived like a princess with Daddy raking in millions and that I, the product of her womb, was living the life that she had been denied.

I did not like this woman who made fun of my teddy bear, my pretty clothes, and my loose hair. She thought my hair should be braided. Sometimes she braided it herself, so tightly that it would leave me with a frozen, surprised look, elf-like eyes, and a headache. I was scared of my mother. I began crying whenever it was time to see her. I was told she loved me, but I did not need this particular kind of love—an hour of yelling and sharp one-way conversations that left me traumatized. She was a mess, and ours was the personification of a difficult relationship between a mother and her daughter. She would sometimes speak of her life, which often would end with her crying and me feeling scared. She showed me marks on her body where someone within her household had hit her and left a mark on her pale skin. The stitch marks she showed me looked like visible marks drawn in by a child. I had nightmares from the scars alone. My father demanded that our meetings be supervised and that only appropriate conversation be shared with me. The court rejected the appeal, and I continued to suffer through my weekly meetings.

One day, my father arranged for my mother to have an all-day, unsupervised visit because he had to attend a convention during the day and stay for dinner in the evening. As soon as he left, my mother went up to his room and opened his safe, the pass code for which was my birth date. Even I, a mere five-year-old, knew the combination. I saw her take out passports; she selected mine and set my father's on fire in the metal dustbin. There were wads of cash in the safe, which she dropped into her open bag. She looked through the papers, found my medical file, and pushed it into her big brown bag. It was all over in minutes. She called someone from the bedroom phone and then grabbed me and walked hurriedly out of the apartment and across the street toward a car with Uncle Adam in the driver's seat. As we drove off, I grew scared, asking to speak to my father and beginning to cry. I wanted to go home, which I began requesting in a higher tone with more fear, over and over until my mother gave me a pinch on my thigh that made me scream with pain.

"We were supposed to stay home," I cried. "Nanny Delphine will be worried. She will notice we are gone and tell Papa. I could just stay home."

"Be quiet and don't you dare create a fuss," said my mother. She had her hair cut in a short, neat bob. She wore a hat over it because the weather was frosty cold that winter. She put a long, thin finger with a ruby ring on it to her lips and shushed me. "I don't want to hear a peep the whole trip."

She was being especially rough that morning, even for her. I whimpered and felt scared. Tears ran down my face and I slowly began bawling. She slapped me on one cheek, and then Uncle Adam yelled that my cheeks would show signs of physical abuse. So she hit me again on the other cheek with less anger because she needed both cheeks to look a dark rose color to not attract attention to them.

"Don't miss the turn and don't get stuck in traffic," she snapped at her brother.

Cars honked. Uncle Adam lowered the window and yelled at another driver. I was in the back seat biting my tongue and trying to hold back the tears. Mother fished through her bag for something and then asked Uncle Adam for a cigarette. He passed her one, but she could not find a lighter so she used his cigarette to light hers.

"Mother, where are we going?" I asked, worried I was going to be smacked.

"Home," she huffed.

I had no idea what she was talking about. We were going farther and farther away from anything that looked familiar. I would tell Papa everything: that Mother hit me twice and yelled at me, and that her smoke made my eyes itch, teary and red.

I did not realize we were on the way to the airport. My mother gave me a pill to take. She said it would help with motion sickness, but it made me so tired that I soon drifted off to sleep. My mother carried me through the security checkpoints where of course I was unable to protest my kidnapping or create a ruckus.

I was drugged for the entire flight. When I awoke, I was in a hot, noisy car that was being driven very fast. My stomach was churning and I needed to use the bathroom. I noticed that one door was held to the vehicle with a plastic rope. I could see the sandy road pass by quickly underneath. White sand covered the floorboard. I counted seven people, including myself, scrunched in the car. Uncle Adam was not among them. It seemed that he had stayed behind in New York.

"I need to go to the bathroom," I said. "Please."

I began trembling. I was afraid if I wet myself she would hit me again. There was a truck ahead of us painted more colors than a rainbow. The car pulled over, and Mother took me by the hand and walked me down the dirt road. When we reached a tall tree, she told me to stop. She expected me to go to the toilet then and there, but I was too nervous. I had never gone to the toilet on an open field of sand, stones, and a few trees. We headed back to the car. I asked when I was going home.

"Enough!" she snapped. "You are staying with me now."

"But what about Papa?" I asked. I thought about how Papa used to call her and would then come to collect me. That always pacified me, and I always went home in the end. As much as I was scared, I just as much expected someone to come collect me and take me home. My mother did not answer, and we got back in the car.

The scenery outside the windows was a never-ending desert of stark white. The road seemed to go on forever. Then there appeared on the horizon a metropolis that looked just like the skyline of New York and I thought we were still in America. Or perhaps in California. I fell asleep and when I awoke, the road still looked the same. I recalled the story of Hansel and Gretel and tried to leave marks along the way, but this road was simply too long for me to remember. Tears streamed down my cheeks as I realized I was far from home and might never see my father again.

As an American girl, I only spoke English and I could not understand the language of the people in the car. The driver was wearing a white short-sleeve shirt and smoked continuously. A large, brunette lady holding a baby in her fat arms sat across from him. She must have gotten out whilst I was asleep. I thought I was in Texas due to the terrain and believed that if I went to a police officer he would take me back to New York. The "Texans" spoke loudly and my mother yelled at them whenever she would pay and haggle. I kept looking for a police officer, but I could not see any.

After several hours of driving we arrived at a small hut made of mud, wood, stone and hay. A large cow and an ox with exaggeratedly long, curled horns grazed outside. My mother ushered me into the hut. This, she said, was my new home. The floor was dirt, covered with straw mats. Dark curtains blotted out the sunlight. There was no air conditioner, only a fan that buzzed loudly. Flies flew in and out under the loose-fitting door. My mother did not seem to mind. Back home, she would have killed them with a flyswatter while complaining bitterly about their filth. Here she did not even bother to shoo them away. The roof had holes, and during the afternoons the rays of sunlight would reveal the swirling dust circulating inside the hut. During the winter months, we would add an extra layer of mud to the outside of the hut to help keep us dry, but the cold was a biting frost that knew no mercy. The blankets did not keep me warm, and I took comfort in the cats sleeping in my bed, as I was grateful for the warmth from their fur and body heat.

I kept hoping that it was all a bad dream and that I would eventually wake up in Central Park. The days dragged on. With time, I realized that the language spoken was not English or Spanish, but Arabic. This was a whole new alphabet. I finally realized that I was all the way in Egypt, the land of mummies and pyramids, and I was afraid of both.

We lived close to a river that stemmed from the Nile, but there were no proper roads, only sandy trails left by people going back and forth for their livelihood. Our electricity came from a wire buried a few inches under the earth. People dressed colorfully and smiled with big teeth. Many people had crooked or broken teeth that my father could have easily fixed, but he was far away—another life away. I had originally hoped that Mother's visiting day would end. But months passed. I prayed when I woke, I prayed when I ate, and I prayed before I went to sleep for my father to call, to come and save me. I stopped asking when I would go home after Mother broke my rib by kicking me. I had a purple-and-blue bruise on my body for weeks afterwards. I became a regular patient at the hospital, and my mother would make fun of what a clumsy girl I was.

I began to learn how to treat my wounds myself because Mother's beatings got harder as financial times got tougher. Every day I expected my Papa to show up at the door, at the fork in the road, at the fruit seller's. Every tourist looked like Papa, and I would try speaking to them in English. My mother would follow and laugh me off as too much of a dreamer, saying, "We used to live in the States, and now my daughter thinks that just because she was born there she is an American."

No one believed me. I felt like I was drowning, with no one acknowledging that I was slowly sinking into a cold, dark, murky grave. It took me some time until I learned to speak Arabic. Only the sellers at the large villages spoke English along with several other languages spoken by tourists. Some were even illiterate but still spoke like music in different languages.

Someone in the playground told me that pyramids were gigantic graveyards for the kings—the pharaohs of Egypt. Egypt scared me, and my biological mother scared me even more. She sometimes hit me so hard in public that I would bleed. God forbid if someone should interfere, because she would lose her mind and say to me, "You are forcing my hand! Why could you not be a good and obedient child?"

Only, I was. I listened to what she ordered me to do but, being a child, when hungry I could not help but cry. Crying would multiply my beatings. She used her hands at first, then shoes, sticks and sometimes a metal bar, but that would make me bleed and left marks so she stopped after the village elder interfered. She tried to explain why she would act so aggressively with me to the villagers, but I was a young, gentle, and scared child and no one ever interfered because "Mommy knows best." Even if it meant I had to go to school with a cut lip, black eye, or a limp. Once she broke my finger in the morning when I dropped my spoon. I was afraid to cry at home, but I cried in writing class in school.

My mother's mother lived a few houses down and came to see us every day. She had brilliant blue eyes and came from "old money," which according to Mother meant that she was penniless and lazy. Whenever she visited, she would end up arguing with my mother about her behavior. Still, she was excited about meeting me, and I tried to explain to her that I needed to go back to the United States and to Papa. I even invited her to join me in my home in the States. She would laugh and say she was home, that Egypt was home, too. She tried to convince me to stay, but when she became upset would begin speaking sternly, so there were limits to what I was comfortable expressing with her.

For the most part, she was patient and kind with me and we would sit for hours reading stories from the three books we had for children. One was *Little Red Riding Hood*, one was a picture book of Cinderella, and the third was *One Thousand and One Nights*. That was a big book with no pictures, so I never bothered opening it on my own. Yet, I did not mind it being read to me at night. It was my whimsical haven, a sanctuary away from the mud hut. I would shut my eyes and imagine taking Aladdin's flying carpet to go shopping with Papa at the big toy stores, or saying "Open sesame" and being able to go back to my bedroom with crispy sheets and a bed of fluff. Nighttime was my sanctuary away from poverty, insects, and beatings.

School was a short walk away in the village and I was quick and hardworking but soon fell behind in my studies because I was not native to the local dialect. I desperately asked teachers, shopkeepers, and even people on the street to contact my father in America, but my pleas landed on deaf ears. People did not understand my pain. How could they? They were staring at this scrawny child who was always whining that she wanted to go to Amreeka and thought her own origin was a mistake. Eventually, I made friends with other children in the school who calmed my fears by playing with me. They were kind and chatty once I deciphered the language with hand gestures and expressions. They ended up becoming a blessing.

Still, I felt like a lost tourist with no passport. Once, I saw young American tourists dressed in military clothes and I went to them, begging them to take me home. "Please tell my Papa I am in Egypt! He is looking for me. I swear."

I was so excited and hoped that they would reach him. I told them his name was Dr Sammy Saad; he was a dentist on the Upper East Side of New York and drove a black Chevrolet. I was his daughter. My mother had taken me away from him, and I had not seen him in years. I said that I needed to go home and that I missed him. My mother showed up and quietly and firmly took my hand. I froze and went quiet.

"My child is a little excited that she has seen Americans," said Mother. She smiled weakly and continued chatting lightly with the tourists. "We went to Disneyland and we had a wonderful time. We hope to go back when she is older." She offered them a cigarette as she helped herself to one. They instantly became her friends. I saw my hopes go up in smoke. They dismissed me as an excited and eccentric child and walked away, thanking Mother for the cigarettes and wishing to see me in America once again.

She waited until we got home and then smacked me with a clay bowl. The bowl broke, and I fell on the floor and could not stand up. My eyes were semi-opened and she thought me dead. I was frail, thin, and already my head had been hit one too many times. It did not hurt. I had stopped feeling anything. I felt cool and collected, as if I were floating on clouds. I stopped caring and just blanked out. She yelled, but I could not comprehend what she was saying. She kicked me, and I think she expected me to get up, but I could not. My grandmother entered to witness Mother kicking the small, frail, unmoving body of her grandchild with a slowly growing pool of blood seeping from her tightly-braided head. I was bleeding from my ears and nose.

I was taken to Aswan University Hospital, the main hospital amongst the villages of southern Egypt. This time it was serious. I could not wake up properly. My vision was blurred and I kept fainting. The headache left me irritable and restless, and I would vomit air and bubbles because there was nothing in my digestive tract to begin with. I was drowsy and drunken-looking all the time. My speech was slurred and I could not get up, nor did I feel inclined to do so. I was breathing, but barely. Mother was worried that she had gone too far. She cried and wailed. I was a boiled cabbage, a vegetating human child in her arms.

Trauma to the skull had resulted in a loss of consciousness. My pupils were of unequal size. My limbs were limp, and I did not flinch. My temperature was dropping, and I could feel my life slipping away.

"You killed her, you crazy, cruel woman," my grandmother whimpered, rocking back and forth in sorrow and bitterly eyeing her daughter. "You should have left her with her father. God will never forgive you. Never. You killed a baby. You monster!"

"Stop it," said Mother. She was nervous. She had miscalculated the strength of the blow, not thinking a clay bowl would crack my skull.

"How was I to know!" she shouted. Her voice broke and she began praying. "I didn't mean to hurt her. She never shuts up about wanting to go home. She belongs with me. Sammy isn't helping, either. I thought he would. I can't afford to keep her anymore. He's against me, you're against me, and the whole world is against me!"

"You should have let her be with her father," said Grandmother. "You can't afford to feed yourself and yet you go ahead and take the child, and now we have two starving fools!"

"Hush, you'll embarrass me. She just had a coconut fall on her head. Stick to the story. I could go to prison if she dies! Oh my God! I won't last a week in there. Mother, promise me you will stick to the story. You saw the coconut fall on her head and I was in the house and then . . . and then I came out. I was nowhere around when this happened."

"Silence, before another lie throws you into the deepest pit of hell, you devil." Grandmother was a firm woman. She had studied Arabic literature and had taught in the local school, but now was collecting her pension and tending to her chickens, ducks and a small group of widows and mothers who stopped by every afternoon for tea.

"Mother, please." My mother pleaded for her own life as mine was slipping away. I stared at the hospital ceiling as her tears fell on my cheeks.

"Things have to change from now on," said Grandmother. "Everything is going to be all right, but you have to change."

The doctors were worried that I had suffered a spinal injury. Upon reviewing the x-ray, they said I had a cracked skull. The doctors inquired how the injury occurred. The coconut story was presented, and I feebly agreed. Better to be with the devil you know than the devil you do not. I was afraid of foster care, as I had seen too many smacked and scarred foster children in the hospital who shared their own tales of woe. I did not want to join them.

I chose to stay silent, as it seemed that I was allowed some peace if I remained so. Mother and Grandmother were ushered into the doctor's clinic and shown my skull x-ray on the screen, revealing a hairline crack. They then came back to my bed in the children's ward and spoke more about my condition. It was a concussion. The doctors explained to them that I would suffer from headaches and cognitive changes, which meant I would feel like I was in a fog. Emotional and behavioral changes were regarded as a further possibility and my sleep would be disturbed.

I was hospitalized for a long time, and the nurses asked me why I had so many bruises, cuts, and scars. I chose not to say anything because Mother might hit me with a rock and I might never wake up next time. I was quiet about wanting to go back to the United States but could not help mentioning that I knew the Disney characters and places in America and most obviously had an American accent.

My mother called my father, hoping he would continue to support me financially even after she had kidnapped me. He in turn called it blackmail and emotional extortion, refusing to be forced into funding a scheme concocted so she could bleed him dry. He was beside himself with grief and yelled over the phone that I could die of malaria or one of a hundred other diseases I was not vaccinated for. He was right. I had malaria several times when I was in Egypt. Furthermore, I was still under his custody and it was not Mother's legal right to take me away. He vowed to come and find me and take me back, but Mother threatened to hurt me if he tried. He became as cold and hard to her as he had been warm and loving to me. Mother was so intimidated by his outbursts that she stopped calling altogether. Father was lost to me for over thirteen years. I did not know a number to call him on and soon had forgotten the details of my address, schools, and the faces and names of my friends.

After I was released from the hospital, I returned to high school. When I graduated, I wanted to go to a good university, but my mother could not afford to send me. She collected the courage to speak with my father and ask him to sponsor me. He agreed to pay for my tuition, books, and fees on one condition: that I would stay with him the entire summer before my first semester started. Overcome with joy, I cried harder than I did when I was first kidnapped. I felt wings sprout on my shoulders, ready to fly me home. I would go back and never return to Egypt. I just needed to keep my thoughts, dreams, and hopes to myself until I was back with Papa.

My father had remarried and moved to California with his new wife. They received me with hugs, kisses and two kids who said they were my sister and brother. I said hello to the young children, as I did not want to be rude, but they were complete strangers to me. My room was furnished exactly as my room in New York had been thirteen years earlier. Father had kept all of my things. My teddy bear was untouched, my musical carousel was in its place on my dresser, and my clothes were hanging in the closet, waiting for me to come back and wear them. My drawings and paintings hung on the walls with small, colored ribbons. My school portraits were hung around the room, perhaps to force my absent presence to be in it. I smelled the scent of lavender on the quilt and remembered the good old times. I felt like Snow White, waking after years of sleep. And yet, my happy ending came with a bitter realization: My father had moved on, and I had not. He was happily married with two children who had compensated for my loss. He simply did not know how to communicate with me anymore. I felt cheated and forgotten. Three new members had taken up my spot in my father's heart. The youngest even reminded me of myself, as I had been abducted at roughly the same age.

I was an adult now, a young woman, with many unanswered questions. Why had he not looked harder for me after my mother took me away? I planned to tell him all about the pain I had endured—the beatings, the feverish nights, the hot days, the cruel taunts of children who did not believe my father was successful and rich, the lonely nights without his stories and kisses goodnight. But I said nothing. I felt my presence in his new life was an interruption because everything was perfectly set for the family that had taken over what was once mine.

I had forgotten the once-familiar tongue and spoke English with a foreign accent. I saw the same lack of acceptance that I had received from the kids at school when I had arrived in Egypt. I was poor then, but I was poorer now. Even when my father gave me money, I felt everyone looked down on me, like I was the adopted charity case. I was a stranger in my own home. A tornado had swept through my safe cottage, wreaking havoc and leaving me to collect the shards of broken memories that left my fingers bloody. I felt raped, taken, abducted. I was lost on so many levels. My home was not mine anymore. My father was not the same person; he was older, and I was no longer his princess. I was an interruption to his life. I did not want to be that. I just wanted to come home, but I felt that I had to tread softly, as if everyone regarded me as a majestic guest. I sensed coyness in the way that everyone was speaking to me. I was the precious china doll that was lost in the post and finally delivered, only too late, long after the birthday or Christmas, long after the days of beauty and play times.

In Egypt I nearly had been killed for wanting to speak my mind. And there I was, in free America, but could not vocalize the demon's voice that was burning me from the inside. I would cry at how broken I was, and how gentle and happy the children were. They were so innocent and easily pleased, but I, who was once the same, had endured too many fractures and emotional scars, leaving my heart deaf to the things that once made it sing. My mind was not the same; my heart was not the same; nothing was the same. Life goes on, or so they say, but my life had come to an abrupt and rude halt, and I wanted to go back home. Only home was not home anymore.

The weather was beautiful but I could not enjoy the sun, the gentle summer breeze, or the beach. Malibu Beach was every sun-loving creature's heaven, but I felt cold the whole summer holiday. There was no space in the car for me, and they had a big dog that I was afraid of. My brother Ramsey told me that the dog was part Irish Wolfhound, a breed used in the past to hunt deer and wolves, and that he was strong enough to carry him on his back when he was younger. The dog would lick me all the time and I could almost swear that his licking me was a teaser for his midnight feast of me. I realized that my thoughts were running wild and made the conscious effort to try not to be morbid and stop putting grotesque masks on every sweet face that came my way.

It felt awkward for my father to have his dinner on the sofa while I sat with his wife and two children at the dinner table that could only seat four. The children were excited that they had a half-sister from the land of the pharaohs and pyramids. They asked me all of the tourist questions about the mummies, the pyramids, the gold, and of course about the terrorists. I told them that I never saw any. We had discussions about religion, politics, and freedom of speech in the West versus the Middle East. They wanted to come visit me in Cairo, and I encouraged them to. I had no friend I could confide my mad situation to. I was finally home, which was exactly what I had wanted, yet I could not wait to leave. I booked my flight back to Egypt and left a week early because I felt choked in this candy-floss happy land, simply because it was not mine anymore. The weather had been sunny; the food, delicious; the people, friendly; but I always felt like the odd one out. The nightmares of the suffering I had endured never left me. These children, along with Papa and my new stepmother, were untainted and unmarked and had not seen the things that would shatter the innocence in their souls.

I spent the vacation happily, but was even happier to return to Mother Egypt. I buried myself in her bosom and began to count my blessings that I had made friends along my troubled road. I moved from southern Egypt to northern Egypt and settled in Cairo to attend university. The metropolis was always bustling and alive, throbbing with life and excitement. Every corner was a new discovery. The people were so diverse and the professors so enlightened they seemed like walking, dusty encyclopedias, as most refused to retire at old age. There were people from all over the world in this bustling metropolis, and the walls would sing the songs of history of thousands of years. Everyone in Cairo had a tale of woe and love, and everyone was eager to tell every stranger their story or someone's story or their own country's story for the sake of storytelling. It was poignant and dusty, an older kind of beauty that held its allure timelessly. People worked very hard in Cairo and the energy of the unified spirit of being from one of the oldest civilizations on Earth made my heart beat faster. I loved America, but Egypt was calling for me. It was my mother— not my biological mother, but my earth mother.

I began working for charities on Fridays and they were my therapy, a place where I could heal by helping other people. I felt as if I was repairing an unset broken rib from old times. I was grateful for the opportunity and I matured and took up responsibilities in university and in clubs. My social life flourished. I enjoyed my popularity, and life was finally beginning to smile down upon me.

The university was a city of lights, holding the promise of worlds of adventure and exploration. The students were of different colors, ages, and nationalities but all agreed that the café opposite the university had the best coffee and tea in the world. Turki, the loud bagel seller opposite the café, certainly had magic baked into his bagels, and they were perfect for breakfast, lunch, or dinner. He swore that his recipe had been handed down from generation to generation, originating from his ancestors: Turks, he claimed, because he had blue eyes. He said that he was named Turki because he had Turkish roots.

The boys would make fun of his hair because it was ridiculously curly and stood like pyramids on each side of his head, where a *taqia* sat covering his shiny forehead. His curly hair was matched by his curly eyelashes, and he had full lips with a flat nose and a square face. Whenever people asked him about where in the world he got his colored eyes, he would gloat and say he had been offered a role in a movie because he was so handsome, blessings be to Him. He would smile and show us his big white teeth from which he usually had a *meswak* stick protruding—the Arabic toothbrush high in fluoride, whose gentle bristles act as such an excellent oral cleaner that the Muslim Prophet, Peace Be Upon Him, advised its use over 1,400 years ago. Turki stood tall and broad in his grey striped *galabya*, his daily uniform, which seemed to host a world of accessories and change from across the continents.

The richness of the air in Cairo made the locals addicted to walking its roads. It is said the Nile is bewitched: Once you drink from its waters, you must return. It was my home now, and in it I found my solace.

My relationship with my mother was the same when I returned from America. We moved out of the mud hut and into an apartment in Cairo for high school and university students. We lived in poverty, sleeping in the same bed and buying only the cheapest food, which always left us feeling like we had not had enough. My mother struggled between jobs that never paid enough. Her tantrums got worse with age.

Once she beat me so hard that I was hospitalized, again. I could not go to university for several days because the shaking train to university rattled my broken ribs and hurt me. I had internal bleeding that left me so bruised I looked like I had been in a car accident. I was wearing a neck brace, and my arm was in a sling. My eye was black, my lip had a cut, and my cheek had a purple bruise with two stitches. The students all guessed car accident; there was no other explanation. It was easy to agree because I felt like a bus had hit me. One of my professors noticed my bruises and the pain that I was in, and insisted that she be allowed to help me. She saw it as her duty to inquire who or what the culprit was. She wanted to find a solution, and I sensed the sincerity in her voice. When I told her Mother was beating me at home, she reacted calmly. She had seen such things before. She took it into her hands to contact my father and ask him to put me up in the university dormitory. Another angel, another day, another blessing in disguise. God had always watched over me and guided me to safety, allowing people to protect me, take care of me, and help me by becoming my sisters, mothers, brothers, and fathers. The Lord works in mysterious ways.

None of my friends knew how bad my situation was. I disguised the unpleasantness in my home by refusing all visitors, saying that my mother was away in the south tending to my ailing grandmother. I did not want my friends to witness her cruel sarcasm toward me or her acid comments about those who were better off than we were. Her cutting sense of humor would insult my old schoolmates and scare even the bravest of my mates away. Friends are the family you choose to help you go through your day-to-day battles, and they were all I had in this world.

Once I began living on campus, life began to get easier for me. I took some odd jobs that helped me socially as well as academically and provided a foundation for future jobs. I found that I had many good friends who stood by me, even when they secretly did not believe that my father was rich when I first came to Egypt as a child. I found sisters in the girls' dorms who became soul mates, mountains of strength and support for every lost or lonely soul. The spirit of unity is the strongest of all in Egypt. The people have a utopian belief that one must always be idealistic and that people will do unto you as you do unto them.

It is a strange reality that when fate robs you of something, God in return sends you angels in disguise that make life worth living. I found my peace in the little things such as the kindness of Turki, who would hand me a bun when I did not have enough to pay for it, just because I was a regular customer. The tragic comedy that was my life became easier when I accepted that this was my luck, and I truly began to enjoy everything that came my way—the good, the bad and the ugly. The good, such as how popular I became with my peers thanks to the roles I played in the university community in terms of studies, clubs, and charity. The bad, such as how emotionally detached from my parents I had become, so much so that I formed my own new family from the friends that I had chosen as my own. The ugly, which was that I was poor in a private and expensive university. At the same time, I was rich with friends who stood by my side in studies, projects, trips, gatherings and odd jobs, always making room for me in their car, their home and at their table when I needed it. I was settled into my own little nest. It was going to be all right.

God is merciful, and I am grateful for everything He has given me. With that realization, I dusted off my past and got up to face the world. I ventured into the business of marketing and events, and currently sit as a successful executive. I believe that in our field of passion, fashion, and madness you almost need to have a personal catastrophe simply to be able to deal with the constant instability. And I am just the person to deal with it now because my history has created in me a savvy mountain that can brave any storm with a smile.

I have not seen my mother in years, as I have moved to Arabia. I go to see my father every Christmas, Easter, and summer break in the States. My siblings now do freelance work in Arabia and come to see me regularly. We have become fast friends. We are all older, and I am more comfortable hosting them. I took them to Cairo and enjoyed their innocence and amazement as they discovered Egypt. I went to the Pyramids for the first time with them, because it is something only tourists do, not the locals. We rode horses at the Haram area, near the Pyramids, after the mile-long graves. People actually live inside the cemeteries, and it was strange seeing them come out of the graves like they were underground homes with large roofs. I wondered how these children could come out of the graves, smiling. That was life in Egypt.

Life in Death.

The fear of nothing.

Life's melody.

I am happy and strong, and most importantly grateful that I am a survivor of life.

Thank you, Egypt.

Bleeding Freedom

B LOOD TRICKLED DOWN MY forehead as the prison guard shaved off my long locks of mahogany hair. My lip was split, and a slow stream of warm, sticky blood was running down my face to my neck. He was using a rusty, broken straight razor that had cut many women before me and would cut many more after me. He said it was the effective way of punishing defiant women. He claimed it was the Islamic way of doing things. But I knew the holy verses, and this man was inventing his own religion in the name of defiance. All I had wanted to do was vote, to have a voice, to exercise my individual right, to take my proper place in society.

I, Jameela, a Muslim half-Arab, half-Berber Algerian, was bubbling over with freedom ideologies and bursting with ideas to help develop the country and encourage us as its citizens to grow and express ourselves. We had suffered under the tyranny of injustice for decades; our nation's death toll under the French was one million martyrs. The attitude of the French toward my people was summed up by Lieutenant-Colonel de Montagnac, who wrote to a friend in 1843:

> *I personally warn all good soldiers whom I have the honor*
> *to lead that if they happen to bring me a living Arab, they*

233

will receive a beating with the flat of the saber . . . This is
how, my dear friend, we must make war against Arabs: kill
all men over the age of fifteen, take all their women and
children, load them onto naval vessels, and send them to the
Marquesas Islands or elsewhere. In one word, annihilate all
who will not crawl beneath our feet like dogs.

Under the French, Muslims made up ninety percent of the population but earned only twenty percent of the nation's income.

Believing the European tradition to be vastly superior to any other, the French eradicated Arabic studies, replacing them with an entirely French curriculum. Algerians were not allowed to speak or write in their native languages, Arabic and Berber.

Although champions of liberty and democracy for their own people, the French created a quasi-apartheid system in Algeria. Even as late as 1947, when the Algerian Assembly was created, half of its members represented the 1.1 million non-Muslim Algerians with the other half representing all of the 6.85 million Muslims.

The under-representation of Algerian Muslims in the Assembly was bitterly resented, especially considering that during World War II, Muslims had made up more than half of the reconstituted French Army. These Algerian fighters in the French Expeditionary Corps helped to liberate parts of Italy, Germany, and France itself.

While demonstrating for their political rights in Sétif in May 1945, the Muslim Algerians clashed with police officers. About 100 police officers were killed in the riots. In retaliation, the French army killed 6,000 Muslim Algerians.

French rule did come to an end eventually, but 132 years under the lash of the French oppressors left scars on our nation. Algeria and its inhabitants were left struggling to rediscover their own identity, language, and destiny. Even people who do not believe in or know of God sometimes pray to a deity in their hour of need. The nation was struggling to find its roots, and the new shoots it sent out trembled with every brush of the wind. Algeria was at war with its own people, who were confused and suffering the consequences of a cultural invasion.

My story took place against this backdrop of repression and its aftermath. I was top of my secondary school class and excelled in all of my subjects. I was nominated by my peers to be prefect, the next celebrated "fingerprint" in the nation—destined to be a doctor, a scientist, or an engineer who would make a mark on the nation and help my fellow citizens forget about the shackles of France. It did not register in my mind that being female made me inferior in any way or any less likely to run for president of my nation had I wanted to do so.

At seventeen, we are at our most rebellious and invincible stage. We have the energy to defy tanks and governments, mothers and fathers, strangers and rabid dogs, presidents and even men with guns they are not afraid to use. I was seventeen when a mad regime took over Algeria; I was at the frontlines of the anti-regime protest movement. I spoke out in public. For my defiance, I was put into prison and my head was shaven. My family had to pay bribes to have me released. Only my family's name and money saved me from receiving heavy beatings and being thrown into a cell with a forgotten lock and rusted key. Others were not so lucky.

The day after my release, my family flew me to neighboring Tunisia, to stay with a cousin. I was ashamed of my shaved head and the scars that the blunt razor left. My parents were afraid of the repercussions that could follow my release, as I had stood first in line against the regime that took over Algeria by storm.

Before I left, my family told me that they had arranged for me to marry an educated man with a promising future. I asked at least to see a picture of my future husband, but they refused to show me anything so I would not be distracted from my education and career.

After spending a week in Tunisia, I was scheduled to fly to Paris to attend college. Despite France's history of occupation in Algeria, I could not wait to return to Paris, which was two hours but seemed ten centuries away from the madmen who now persecuted me in Algeria. I had no resentment toward the French, for the French in Algeria were soldiers persecuted almost as much as we were. It was the war-mongering egoist at the top who wanted to control more than what was rightly his. The French friends I had were good to me and received me kindly.

After waiting for the women with children and the disabled to board the aircraft, I walked down the gangway and entered the cabin. The flight attendant directed me to my seat. When I reached my row, I saw a handsome gentleman occupying my seat. I placed my carry-on luggage in the overhead bin, then reached into my bag and took out my boarding pass. "I'm afraid you're in my seat," I said, indicating the seat number on my boarding pass. "I always get an aisle seat," I explained.

With that, the stranger stood up and smiled. "You are even more beautiful in person than in your pictures," he said.

"Excuse me?" I said. "I'm afraid you have confused me with someone else."

"I certainly hope not," said the man with an admiring gaze.

The way he was staring made me uncomfortable, but the girl who had stood up to a regime was not afraid to stand up to a leering businessman. "Here is my seat number," I said, holding out my boarding pass.

"Of course, my dear, if you wish to have the aisle seat, it's yours. I was raised to believe that a man should walk and sit to the outside of his wife, to protect her. But after all, this is not a street in Algiers, and these are not the Middle Ages." He forced a laugh as if to break the tension.

"Wife? Sir, I do not know who you are or why you are talking to me like this, but I find it extremely disrespectful and upsetting. I'm sorry if I sound angry, but I happen to be engaged and I do not appreciate your behavior. If you won't agree to stop speaking to me for the duration of the flight, I will ask for another seat."

The man looked shocked. "You're Jameela, right?" he asked.

I searched his eyes for signs of a joke, or malice. All I saw was confusion. "Yes," I said. "And you are?"

"I am Kareem," said the man with obvious relief. "Your husband."

I stood there in disbelief. My family had forgotten to mention that they had married me off without telling me!

"Please take your seat," said the flight attendant, coming down the aisle.

I had no choice but to sit next to him. I began to cry. Soft tears turned to hard sobs as I tried to figure out how my family could have done this to me.

My husband tried to calm me down. He told me he was not a bad man. He was highly educated, having attended universities in the United States and Canada. He promised to take me there to show me the sights—New York City, Niagara Falls, Washington DC, the Rocky Mountains.

It didn't help. I cried through the whole trip. He tried to distract me with pictures of our house in Paris, our pet dog, our plants and neighbors, and his workplace. He told me how he would drop me at the university and collect me after work. It all seemed surreal. I simply sat there, sniffling and gulping coffee, wanting to snap out of this bad dream.

Handsome and educated, Kareem was neither bad nor backward. In all fairness, he seemed like every woman's dream come true. He took my hand and held it throughout the flight. When we arrived in Paris, he checked us into a hotel for our "honeymoon" and led me to our room, holding my hand the whole way. He even carried me over the threshold. He was trying to make me feel special, but as I got ready for bed, I stood in the bathroom, shaking. I was about to give myself to a man I had known only a few hours. I felt like one of those women in a Hollywood movie who goes home with a man after only meeting him in a bar. I was only seventeen, and this was my virginity. This was not how I had imagined my wedding night would be.

Kareem assumed the role of the husband, but as proper as he was, he was short and curt with his emotions, both in conversation and in intimacy. My wedding night was a disappointment, as were the days and nights that followed. I grew lonely, but soon became pregnant. With my babies, my career, and my life, I found my own happiness.

I abandoned my activism in the airport in Algeria. I loved my country, but when you are not recognized and you are not allowed to exist, you can only send your prayers, blessings, and wishes. And surely, in due time, things slowly and painfully came together in a full circle. After things began to go well, I visited Algeria often and was happy at how it was developing.

I excelled in my studies in France, rising to the top of the class. Later, when I was employed, I was one of fifty out of 3,000 applicants accepted to specialize in investment banking and eventually selected to manage my firm's biggest and most important European portfolios. The energy I had put toward my former political activism was now channeled into my career.

I succeeded and prospered professionally, but I felt empty and unsatisfied in my marriage. Despite my disappointment, I held on to the marriage, partly for the convenience of having a father figure for the children and partly so my family could feel satisfied that their daughter had a man to take care of her—something as important to the older generation as it was irrelevant to mine.

Thanks to my business success, my paycheck was larger than my husband's, and I made sure that every franc stayed in the family home. Jealous of my success, my husband reacted by looking for ways to throw his money away. He developed a gambling problem and took a double mortgage out on the house in order to indulge in his hobby.

Fifteen years passed by with their fair share of happy family moments, thanks mainly to my two beautiful sons and our lovely home. But my marriage went from bad to worse. Kareem had two affairs, each of which shook the marriage—the first because I didn't expect it, and the second because after the first one he said it would never happen again. After the second one ended, it hit me that I had never been in love with Kareem. Our marriage was arranged; he was not my choice. We both tried to make the marriage work, especially at the beginning, but sometimes you just cannot succeed.

One day I realized that I was only thirty-two and still had many good years ahead of me. My emotional intelligence simply refused to accept the perennial monotone of an empty marriage. I gathered my courage and asked Kareem for a divorce. He refused and became quite angry.

He was shocked that I even dared to request a divorce, for how could a woman live without her man? He could cheat, but he never expected that his wife would tire of her empty life, pack her bags, and leave. Unheard of. Blasphemous. Immoral. Madness. But then again, I was never one to follow reformative ways, and I divorced him anyway.

Despite the debts that I was left with on Kareem's behalf, the biggest loss was the emotional hole that my two sons now felt without a father figure. Nevertheless, I knew that I had made the right decision.

It took a few grueling years, but eventually I covered the installments, paid off the debts, and owned my home. I had conquered the money mountain and regained my independence, but it was a feat that shook me to my core. I struggled for some time to overcome my feelings of failure and desertion, the guilt that I felt for breaking apart my family. But I knew that I could not let myself be defined by one man, that I had a greater purpose to fulfill. Had it not been for my determination to provide the best for my sons, I might have succumbed to a provincial life in Algeria with my elder siblings and relatives, hidden and safe from any possible scandal that I, a divorcee, could possibly get into. But I defied expectations, as it had always been in my nature to do. The fire that had burned inside me when I was seventeen was rekindled to cleanse, purify, and strengthen my life.

After securing my sons' futures and my own, I left Europe to be closer to my cultural and religious roots: I relocated to Dubai and made it my new homeland. I sold what I could and carved out a new life for myself. I was successful because in Dubai, if you work hard, you are recognized for it and lifted up to where you deserve to be in this world regardless of your gender, race, or religion. I am now a manager of an important bank and I stand tall, proud of who and what I am. I speak the language and enjoy the culture that I, an Algerian-French woman, embrace and love. Life has been hard but fair to me. The Lord giveth and the Lord taketh away. And I regret nothing that I did when my heart longed for it.

I hope we all learn to live the lives we choose for ourselves, not the ones dictated for us by the colonial French, or the extremists, or the family; that we overcome sexism and the nightmares that haunt us, that tie us down to the ghosts of our pasts, that make us live in fear of being on our own and of exploring our future and all that it may hold for us.

As the popular French singer Edith Piaf famously sang, *Je ne regrette rien*.

ACKNOWLEDGEMENTS

I would like to thank my mother, Mahra, and father, Dr. Faisal, and all my sisters and brothers for their love and support. Thank you to my grandmother who showed me that it is never too late to follow your dreams.

I want to thank Bradley Steffens for being my biggest support in properly presenting the stories and this book.

I am deeply indebted to the women who have shared their stories of perseverance, survival, and triumph with me. I have protected their identities by changing names, but the events have all happened in the land of the desert.